AF414779

The Avaricious

Also by JoAnn Fastoff

Fiction
Howard Watson Intrigue Series
The Scheduler
The Standing People
The Smoke Ring
The Lie
The Pact
The Gordian Knot

Non-Fiction
You Play Like A Girl
(History of the first Women in Sports)
White Sox
(and other baseball worth mentioning) for Women
Two Years of Heaven
(Stories of Re-kindled Happiness)

The Avaricious
(A Howard Watson Intrigue)

JoAnn Fastoff

The Avaricious (A Howard Watson Intrigue)
© by JoAnn Fastoff, 2022
First edition
Crime-Thriller-Series

All rights reserved. No part of this book may be reproduced, stored in a retrieval system, or transmitted by any means without the written permission of the author. This is a work of fiction. Any resemblance to persons living or dead is strictly coincidental.

Print ISBN 9798218039127
Electronic 9798218040123
Library of Congress Catalog in Publication information in progress

Cover art by Paul Ruane

Published by JoAnn Fastoff
www.joannfastoff.com

The Avaricious is a highly thought-provoking and spellbinding tale of mastery, which fuses true greed with criminal intrigue while leaving the reader captivated from beginning to end.

**D. Darell Dones, PhD.,
former FBI Supervisory Special Agent
(1988-2014); CEO of Dones Global Solutions, LLC.**

In yet another thrilling whodunit, JoAnn Fastoff keeps the reader turning the pages of *The Avaricious* to find the next clues. This is another Howard Watson intrigue you don't want to miss.

**R. Lee Walters,
former FBI Special Agent (1989-2012)**

Readers can read *The Avaricious* without having read the other Howard Watson books first as it stands well on its own, however, I can guarantee that they will want to go back and read the others! *The Avaricious* intrigue is fast-paced and had me reading it in a single sitting. Highly recommended reading!

**Reviewed by Paige Lovitt
for Reader Views (07/2022)**

A neatly tied up FBI sting. Through the action Fastoff exposes ongoing criminal and social issues that are often hidden under the rug. New intrigue and characters that will excite those who have read previous books in this series.

**Keridak Silk,
Author, winner first place short story,
Lakefly Writers Conference 2022**

Acknowledgements

Although *The Avaricious* is a work of fiction, leftover anti-personnel landmines dotted throughout the globe are real. According to the International Coalition to Ban Landmines, over 60 countries and territories have landmines that remain unexploded in the ground.

One hundred sixty-four countries have signed the Anti-Personnel Mine Ban Convention (APMBC). This document is a key UN instrument for combating the use of landmines and reducing their impact. Two years ago, an action plan was drawn up in Oslo, Norway with an ambitious goal: a mine-free world by 2025.

We can only hope this plan works.

JF

***

The Chesapeake Bay waters in the early summer tend to be shimmery, smooth, and gorgeous; the waves white against the deep blue. It holds over 3,600 species of animals and plants supported by its nutrient-rich waters. It is an appealing spot for families, water sports, boating and fishing.

The Piscataway Indigenous man and his adult grandson had been in the boat all morning, their sun-drenched faces now smiling broadly at their great catch of oysters and striped bass. The grandfather glanced up at the tundra swans as they crossed the cloudless sky. He then placed their bountiful catch in three giant ice chests. As he was pulling his net for the day, he noticed a man in the distance hanging on to the rocks of the nearby lighthouse. He glanced around for a boat, something, anything…nothing. He motioned to his grandson to pull in his net. When they inched closer to the lighthouse without running afoul of the rocks, the grandfather realized the man was dead, his mouth was duct-taped, and his hands were tied behind his back. The purple and blue spots on his face and head made it appear as if he had been beaten before his death. The grandson used his cellphone to call the authorities.

***

The Piscataway Nation did not trust the police, and the grandfather did not trust this policeman, with his steely gray eyes, who did not believe that he and his grandson had nothing to do with the stranger washing up on the rocks. After an hour, the man and his grandson were finally free to leave the station. But it took yet another explanation to the Naval Criminal Investigative Service.

"The truth has no versions," the old man told the NCIS.

"Why were we kept there such a long time, Grandfather?" the young man asked as they walked out of the station.

"Because, Billy," the grandfather answered, more than slightly perturbed, "they wanted *their* answer, which we could not give them and will never give them."

They left the station and headed to the grandson's pickup truck. Billy glanced back over his shoulder and saw that the officer was still watching them. The grandfather shook his head.

Billy watched the older man for future reference.

3

"A poor person isn't he who has little, but he who needs a lot."
- Proverb

PART ONE

Baltimore, Maryland

Dr. Tadeo Tran and his colleague Dr. Ruby Ha, both of Vietnamese descent, were discussing in front of ten other people in a store-front office the need for the removal of antipersonnel explosives in Vietnam.

"Our organization," Dr. Ha persisted adamantly, "returns the land to productive use, cultivating a brighter future for the children and families of Vietnam."

A hand went in the air. Dr. Ha pointed to the hand.

"Are you saying," the man began, "that there are still landmines in Vietnam?"

Dr. Tran answered, unsmiling. "In Vietnam alone, leftover landmines and other explosives dropped by the United States have killed over 40,000 people since the end of the war in 1975. Every twenty-two minutes, someone is killed or maimed by a landmine. One-third of the world's countries are littered with landmines, and the State Department estimates that 60 to 75 million landmines remain unexploded in the ground worldwide."

Another hand went in the air. "How long will it take to remove all the leftover mines?"

Dr. Tran answered again, this time slowly. "It may take 300 years for all remaining munitions to be cleared out of Vietnam."

He paused. "In other words, the last Vietnamese person to be killed by an unexploded US munition probably hasn't even been born."

***

FBI Headquarters, Washington, DC

Supervisory Special Agent Howard Watson was pulling in to his parking spot in the underground garage of the J. Edgar Hoover Building when he noticed his boss, Section Chief Alberto Marino, standing outside the elevator. Howard had barely made it out of his car when Marino approached him.

"If you haven't eaten yet, let's grab some breakfast."

Howard knew when Marino called him *at dawn* that something was up.

After finding the quietest section of the employee cafeteria, Marino took a sip of his coffee before he slammed the system. "I know you're going to hate this, but I have to put your unit on a new mission."

Howard stared at his breakfast and waited for the other shoe to drop.

"John wants us to work on a hush-hush basis with the US Army and Maryland State Police to uncover why two scientists working on landmine patents have disappeared."

Howard put his fork down and turned his gaze on Marino. "Al, we just came off a serial killing case less than a month ago. I have paperwork that I haven't submitted for two other cases—forget the Ericksen case. Can't you get Frank or Archie to take this over?"

Marino shook his head. "Sorry, but you and Chief Stanley are tight buddies, and this 'situation' landed in Stanley's lap."

Howard hung his head. "Okay, Al, what situation are we talking about?"

***

Later in the morning, Howard was in his office staring out of his window to the building's inner courtyard grounds when he noticed the employees scrambling to get inside from the sudden downpour. He was trying his best not to be suckered in by the rhythmic beat of the drizzling rain against the window. The sound of his staff arriving brought him back to the present.

Tim Yamamoto, Ahmad Waverly, Brett Hamilton, and Kevin Lee trudged through his heavy oak door like people who didn't want to know what would happen next. He understood fully why no one was smiling and knew it had nothing to do with the outside weather. He motioned all the agents to take seats at his round conference table. He took a seat at his desk.

"Guys," he began, looking at his computer screen. "We have a situation in Maryland that deals with two missing top-notch scientists." He then turned to the team. "Before you ask me anything, Jim Stanley, Maryland State Police, who we all know, Gerry Kramer and Terrence Millhouse, FBI Baltimore, and US Army Major General Grace Westwood should be arriving soon. They will be giving us the lowdown on leftover landmines and the black market profiting heavily out of Baltimore Harbor."

"Are you talking about 'Turpentine' Millhouse?" Brett asked.

Howard looked at his screen.

"I don't know about the Turpentine part. You know him, Brett?"

"Oh yeah, I graduated Quantico with him. He's in

Baltimore now, huh?"

"Seems that way. Turpentine?"

Brett could not contain his smile. "Long story. Really smart guy."

Howard's Executive Assistant then announced via his speakerphone that the guests had arrived.

"Thanks, Shareese. Please have someone escort them to Al's conference room."

Howard then called Marino to apprise him of the guests on their way. He looked at the men in his office. "Let's go."

***

The guests were already seated at the long mahogany table when Howard and his team stepped into Marino's conference room. Assistant Director John Fleischman, Marino's boss, was sitting at one end of the table. Howard figured that it must be the head of the table if Fleischman was in the room. Marino was seated near Fleischman. Howard took a seat across from Marino. After introductions were made, Section Chief Gerry Kramer, Millhouse's boss, walked in and quickly took a seat next to Marino. They shook hands.

"Thank you all for agreeing to forego your desks' laundry lists," Fleischman spouted.

No one smiled. After introducing Gerry Kramer, Fleischman opened the meeting. "Major General Westwood, why don't you begin?"

The tall, beautiful, Black woman unfolded herself from her chair. Her uniform proudly displayed the perfectly crafted Army military ribbon and medal racks.

"After working on their prototype for three years," she said with a slight quiver in her voice, "my sister, Dr. Paula Malloy, co-developed with Dr. Antony Serrano a microchip technology to target a 'manageable level 'of finding cluster bombs in Vietnam. The laboratory's specialties include space, physics, material sciences and tactical electronic warfare."

She paused. "Only a select few in the military knew that these two were working on this unbelievably wonderful invention. However, Paula and Tony had been missing for four days when Tony's body washed up on a lighthouse in the Chesapeake Bay. It has now been six days and my sister is still missing. I'm asking for the FBI's help to find my sister."

Fleischman looked in Kramer's direction. He got the hint.

"Since I am just getting up to par on the topic of landmine stockpiling, I'm going to submit humbly to my exceptional staff for authenticity." He looked at Millhouse.

"Again, I am Supervisory Special Agent Terrence Millhouse from FBI Baltimore." He glanced over at Brett, nodded, and smiled. "Although on the surface this looks like an external government problem, Baltimore is assisting for several reasons. One, these are American scientists working on a top-secret patent for the US military and two, a name some of you know—Boris Ramashka— we believe is part of a black market supply chain dealing with landmines."

"The Hyatt Exec?" Howard asked.

"Same one, Agent Watson."

"Who is he working with?" Marino asked.

"A very wealthy banker out of France named Sebastien Mischicot."

"This should be a situation for CIA, not FBI," Fleischman quipped.

"It should be, Director," Millhouse said with little emotion, "and it will be, but for now Ramashka is in Maryland, which is in the United States and therefore FBI territory, and Mischicot is in France, which is CIA."

Fleischman ignored his seemingly sarcastic tone. "Who's the bomb tech from Quantico, and when do we meet him?" Fleischman asked.

"*Her* name is Sandra Callahan," Kramer injected. "She has fifteen years under her belt as an explosives expert and is fluent in French. I believe Agent Watson, Agent Millhouse, and Agent Callahan should get along fine."

Everyone turned in Howard's direction. He offered no confirmation.

"Chief Stanley, what does the State Police know?" Fleischman asked.

After Jim Stanley got over the shock of Fleischman remembering his name, he slid ten pamphlets across and down the table for everyone to peruse.

"Good to see familiar faces," he said with a slight smile. "We have only known about Ramashka for two months because of a tip that he was part of an organization running a profitable back door business in several areas dealing with, you guessed it, leftover landmines. We were not initially interested until two analysts from Department of Defense who worked for the scientists approached us because their bosses had been missing for four days." He poured himself a glass of water from the pitcher on the table. He then adjusted the pamphlet in front of him.

"We didn't brush them off but, to be honest, we thought perhaps the two scientists just ran off together. The analysts assured us that in no way were the scientists involved intimately. They were worried because the scientists had just developed some top-level governmental chip associated with finding landmines. Their concerns were later justified because Dr. Serrano's body washed up in the Chesapeake two days ago. I told them to contact the FBI, specifically you, Howard. If MSP can help the FBI, we're in."

***

FBI Baltimore

Howard and Jim Stanley met at Millhouse's office after lunch. All were seated at his small conference table. While each read the report on the missing scientists, the quiet was so eerie that a needle dropped on the dark green carpet would have echoed.

Walking through the doors, however, was the not-so-quiet chatter emanating from Al Marino and Gerry Kramer. Millhouse bit his lower lip when both men plopped down on his plush, green leather sofa…the sofa he bought personally.

"Guys," Kramer began. "The rumors swirling around Mr. Ramashka at this time have to be treated as rumors. We're talking about an upstanding citizen in Maryland business and philanthropy."

He paused. "However, don't get me wrong, I've been in this job long enough to know that power corrupts."

He looked over at Millhouse. "Terrence, why don't you tell us what you know."

"Sure, Gerry." Millhouse got up from his chair to face everyone. "Vietnam remains one of the world's most contaminated countries, with an estimated 800,000 tons of unexploded bombs, leftover from the war that ended more than forty years ago. And the largest stockpiles of antipersonnel mines are held by China, Russia, Belarus, Ukraine, Italy, India and us. It is difficult to obtain details on the numbers, types, or country of origin of stockpiled mines. And mines have been used predominantly in conflicts between government troops and ethnic armed groups, so the wars in Vietnam and Cambodia have left ample quantities of landmines on the regional black market."

"Now that production and transfer have halted under the Mine Ban Treaty, fewer groups are able to obtain factory-made antipersonnel mines. Some black market entrepreneurs have acquired landmines by stealing them from government stocks or removing them from minefields. And some have made their own improvised landmines from locally available materials."

He looked at each of them. "Do not be naive thinking the US has stayed out of this fray as companies manufacturing antipersonnel landmines included giants such as Daimler-Benz, the Fiat Group, the Daewoo Group, RCA, and General Electric. Yeah, real Americans."

***

Terrence Millhouse grew up in a family of teachers in Atlanta. Both parents and both sides of grandparents were all teachers. His two brothers and his sister were either on the education boards or administrators in the education system in Atlanta. So when Terrence, the youngest sibling, at age twenty-six, announced at the dinner table one Thanksgiving Day that he had been accepted into the FBI Academy, not an eye blinked, nor a smile escaped anyone's face at the dinner table.

His usually articulate well-spoken paternal grandfather was the first to put his fork down

"You gotta be kiddin' us, right?"

To say that anyone was pleased with the announcement would be stretching the truth.

They were barely listening to Terrence, the family's youngest, the National Honors society man, the Morehouse Man, the Howard University Master's in Economics man.

Nope, it didn't go down easy for anyone at the table.

No one in his family and family of friends could comprehend why a smart, handsome, African American man would want to join, in their minds, the white elitist illuminati called the FBI.

No one.

It was hard to explain why he was so excited about the FBI that he ended up stuttering out the justification.

It didn't help one bit…so he gave up and went back to eating.

For the next several weeks until he entered the Academy, young Millhouse went through agony stemming from his family, his friends, and his latest girlfriend.

But, according to all, "Once Terrence made up his mind about something, there was no shaking another way out of him."

***

Millhouse entered The FBI Academy at Quantico, Virginia, and was placed with a roommate named Everett Fischer, a Caucasian man from Georgia…not Atlanta, but Georgia. So to say they had differences of opinion about everything was conservative talk. Both almost immediately asked to be reassigned rooms. Quantico told them, "We are a team, and if you can't get along with each other, then the FBI doesn't want you."

Both men sucked in their egos and attempted to ride it out at least past HELL WEEK, where their mettle was at stake. According to numerous Trainees, though, this is where the story becomes muddled.

Millhouse had been on his way to tactical weapons training when several balloons filled with soapy water "fell" from the sky and landed on him while he was in uniform. He then ran back to his room to change but was written up because he was late for the training. His perfect record, up to that point, was destroyed. When he walked past the mess to return to his room later, the New Agents Trainees stared at him but didn't utter a word.

Only two other Trainees in the class were people of color. Millhouse never believed for a minute that they had anything to do with his humiliation. No one took credit, and Millhouse complained, but Quantico told him to ride it out.

***

Although he was an excellent trainee, Everett Fischer was considered a pompous ass, not only by Millhouse but by numerous other Trainees in the class. Most believed Fischer was related to someone in the upper echelons of the FBI because Quantico seemed to look the other way regarding his several shenanigans. When Fischer, with no seniority whatsoever, requested the FBI Atlanta Office after graduation and got the post, any doubt about his pedigree was removed.

Fischer was running solo one evening in the woods the last week at Quantico. Because the person was wearing a skull cap, mask, and gloves, he could not tell who grabbed him from behind, tied him to the tree, and poured turpentine all over his lower body. After review, the video offered no conclusive evidence. No one ever took credit, but most believed it was Millhouse. Unless Fischer wanted to complain, Quantico considered the case closed. Fischer did not complain.

***

When Howard walked into Marino's office, Marino was staring out his big picture window on to the Washington Mall. He spoke while still staring out the window.

"Howard, have Yamamoto inquire about Callahan. See if she has a screw loose like the rest of those bomb techs outta Quantico. I want to know who we're dealing with in terms of intelligence. Also, find those two analysts. I want to know what they know."

After chuckling slightly, Howard nodded at his request.

"I have Ahmad going over the MSP report on Dr. Serrano, taking special note of time and type of death."

"Good, get those analysts in as soon as possible."

***

Tadeo Tran and Ruby Ha were quite shocked when informed that the FBI wanted to talk with them. They assumed that their involvement with the US Army Scientific Lab was completed. They were not aware of Dr. Serrano's death. When they arrived in Marino's office, Howard, Millhouse, and Jim Stanley were already seated at his conference table. The scientists were offered seats on Marino's sofa. Stanley started the conversation.

"Doctors, you recall our conversation regarding your concern for Drs. Serrano and Malloy in my office?"

Both nodded.

"I'm sorry to report some sad news. Dr. Serrano's body was recovered several days ago in the Chesapeake Waters. We have yet to discover if Dr. Malloy is alive."

Ruby burst into tears. Tadeo, although visibly upset, was able to compose himself while asking for the grizzly details.

After Stanley handed Ruby tissues and a bottled water, he spewed out the sketchy details of Dr. Serrano's death, while continuing with his reporting.

"At this time, the NCIS states that Dr. Serrano's mouth was duct-taped and his wrists bound behind him when his body was pulled out of the water. He had several bruises on his face and the back of his head. It is believed he suffered a heart attack before his body was found in the Chesapeake."

Ruby could not stop the flow of tears. "He…he was such a nice man," she was able to say in between sobs. "He was extremely smart but wasn't condescending. He was newly engaged, and his soon-to-be husband was also a doctor, but the medical kind."

"Did Dr. Serrano or even Dr. Malloy ever mention anything about anyone threatening or harassing them?" Howard asked.

"No," Tadeo answered. "At least not to me."

Ruby stopped crying. "I don't know if this means anything," she said, "but I do remember about a month ago Dr. Malloy saying that a woman asked her in the bathroom of the restaurant where we were having lunch if she ever got claustrophobia working in a lab every day."

"And why was this so strange?" Howard asked.

"Because Dr. Malloy said she didn't know her, and I'd never seen her before either."

Howard filed away this information. He continued the line of questioning.

"When and why did you and Dr. Tran start working for Malloy and Serrano?"

"Both of us," Ruby answered, pointing to herself and Tadeo, "are first-generation Americans, Agent Watson. We were working on drone techniques at Redstone Arsenal in Alabama when the army, specifically Major General Westwood, approached us a year ago to work with the scientists in Baltimore. We were overjoyed as we were also working on our Ph.D. theses focusing on science competitions that foster innovation for the benefit of humanity. In case you didn't know, Vietnam is still saturated with thousands of unexploded mines. Imagine assisting them in their quest to apply robotics technology that would be able to detect unexploded landmines."

She took a drink of water.

"Well, the finished product became a microchip for a landmine spotting system. We were beyond pleased with the prototype, thinking Paula and Tony might even be nominated for the Nobel Prize in Economic Sciences."

Before Ruby could continue, Howard received a text on his phone. He looked at both doctors. "Would you mind if one of my agents joined this meeting? He's my invention guru and dying to meet you both."

Marino looked at Howard. "Waverly?" he asked.

Howard could not contain his smile. "Who else?"

***

Baltimore, Maryland

Both sides of Boris Ramashka's family fled Russia in 1910 and emigrated to America to avoid Jewish persecution. His mother's family landed in Philadelphia, and his father's side landed in New York.

Although Boris's parents were born in America, they never talked about how they met, which left him thinking "Russian Jews were always too damn tight-lipped."

Boris's older brother and sister were born in New York, but Boris and his little sister, who called him Bobo, were born in Maryland, where his parents relocated because the jobs were plentiful.

Young Ramashka was always a piece of work; always into something. He was small for his age, and when he started getting pushed around in the third grade because he was Jewish, he started "buying" bodyguards two to three years older. His older brother and sister thought of him as a thug but a smart one. They were pretty happy that the two of them were five and six years older than Bobo, so they didn't have to attend the same school and constantly keep him out of trouble. Bobo's younger sister adored him…and he loved it.

Ramashka's parents scrimped and saved their money franticly. They were adamant about all of their children going to *and graduating* from college, so Bobo didn't disappoint and graduated from the University of Baltimore with a degree in Business. There, he met a young, ambitious international student named Seffy Mischicot.

***

After graduation from college, Boris Ramashka started working for Hyatt International, and with fantastic advice from Seffy Mischicot, he wisely invested his money in Hyatt International shares. At twenty-eight, he became a millionaire. He then moved to the little town of Crofton, twenty minutes away from his parents in Baltimore and where there were a lot of restaurants and parks. He knew his parents would love the quaint, under-the-radar little place where he could get his side hustle on without a spotlight on his life. The side hustle? Ramashka, and Mischicot, who was now working for Corporate and Investment Banking in France, began to devise a plan to buy up all the leftover landmines in Vietnam and sell them to countries bracing for war.

***

Paris, France

Sebastien Mischicot, or Seffy to family and close friends, was born into a wealthy *Societe Generale* family of bankers. His grandfather and two great-uncles were considered progressive businessmen in the early twentieth century for stepping out of "the box" to offer French mortgages and various borrowing options tailored to meet the needs of ex-pats and non-residents after World War II. It worked effortlessly, and the complete Mischicot family became rich within a decade.

Seffy and his three older brothers were introduced to the banking industry as soon as they could read and count numbers. His brothers all graduated from HEC Paris, one of the world's leading business schools across all programs. Their father gave each a hefty endowment once they graduated. All of Seffy's brothers became richer by investing wisely.

But Seffy, it seemed, wanted more than just a banking background. He could never seem to have enough. He wanted to be more than just rich…he wanted to be crazy rich. His father and mother had given up on trying to counsel Seffy on needs that were not necessary. The Mischicot family had every single financial need Seffy could ever want. But when Seffy decided to attend graduate business school in Baltimore, in the United States, his brothers' flags were up. Why was he going to graduate school in the US? To learn what?

Sebastien was now a "grown man" so any advice was left on deaf ears.

***

Calvert County, Maryland

The landscape of the Piscataway Nation settlement in southern Calvert County consists of a series of historic "longhouses" that can house several families usually headed by a matriarch, single-family trailers, and newly developed housing mostly occupied by younger single people. The Piscataway Indigenous live modestly as farmers, weavers, and fishers. The homes are bordered on the East by the Chesapeake Bay and on the West by the Lower Patuxent River. Farms and vacant land from former tobacco fields dot the area. Although the county has become a fast-growing prosperous neighbor of Washington, DC, those profits have not yet reached the Piscataway Peoples from whom they say the land was taken. A sign which reads "You Are On Stolen Land" is posted prominently outside the settlement entrance.

***

The young Black woman was found deep in the forest at the bottom of Cat Hole Trail, face down in the mud, only yards from the Lower Patuxent River. A group elder deduced that she tripped, fell down the cliff, hit her head on a boulder, and blacked out. She did not have any identification on her except a necklace that held a miniature key. The fall completely ruined the suit and heels she was initially wearing. In addition, her mouth was duct-taped, and her wrists were bound behind her. What was she escaping? Better yet, who was she fleeing?

Six days later, the young woman coughed up blood when she woke up on the worn but spotlessly clean sofa in the open room of a longhouse. She felt throbbing in one ankle, looked down and saw that it was bound tightly. Her head felt as if it weighed twenty pounds, so she laid back down. She could not tell the several concerned-looking people her name. First of all, she couldn't remember it, and secondly, where was she and why was she dressed in these strange clothes?

Those gathered began speaking Algonquin. How did she know this? The chatter ceased when the young man with the sun drenched face walked into the house. He pulled up a chair and sat next to her.

"Miss, my name is Billy Savoy." He then pointed to the group of people around her. "We are of the Piscataway Tribal Nation here in Calvert County. Our elders are happy to report that nothing on you appears to be broken, just a sprained ankle, and we did take care of your busted lip and your bruises. We did not contact the police because we do not know who is your enemy. Who did this to you? Do you remember who tied your wrists and taped your mouth?"

She shook her head. "I have no idea. How long have I been here? Does my family know I'm here?"

"You have been here six days."

He smiled at several women.

"Our mothers have taken care of you. Where is your family? We can contact them for you."

She shook her head again. The tears began flowing.

"I-I don't know. I can't remember. What has happened to me?"

***

Sandra Callahan swept through Marino's doors like she had been there before. Her red hair and freckles seemed on fire. She then shook Marino's hand aggressively but with a smile. Marino couldn't help himself; he knew he was old-school, but he hated aggressive women. It didn't matter that she was good-looking and intelligent…she was feisty. This did not sit well with him.

"My lead agent on this case is Howard Watson, Agent Callahan. He should be…"

At that moment, Howard was walking through Marino's door. Marino exhaled.

"Sorry that I'm tardy, Al. Based on the description, this must be Special Agent Callahan." Howard then reached out his hand to shake hers. She had some firm grip.

"I've been looking forward to meeting you both, but especially you, Agent Watson," she said, almost gushing. "Your cousin Carrie has told me so much about you that I feel as if I already know you."

"So maybe this one time she was being completely honest and that I'm all that."

He and Callahan laughed…but not Marino.

"Agent Callahan," Marino said dryly, "why don't you tell us what you know about black market landmines?"

She and Howard took seats in the empty chairs facing Marino's desk.

"Sure, Chief," she said with a slight smile, quickly fading.

"Accompanied by Russian-backed monies, the growing threat of landmines and improvised explosives in the Central African Republic, or CAR, points to a dangerous shift in a new type of guerrilla war."

"Why is Russia helping CAR," Marino piped in, "especially since they don't give a damn about those people?"

"Terrific question, Chief. Easy enough answer. The Central African Republic is rich in diamonds, gold, oil, and uranium."

Marino offered her a bottled water, which she graciously accepted.

"You see, more than twenty years ago, a global treaty banned the use of landmines targeted at individuals, though Russia did not and has not signed on to the treaty. Conventional Wisdom suggests so-called instructors include Russian mercenaries from various groups and private military companies with combat experience. The impact of these black market landmines on civilians is devastating. They are everywhere—planted on roads and even near schools, and the landmines cut villagers off from peacekeeper patrols and humanitarian help. The mines force people from their homes."

"Where are these so-called mercenaries getting these landmines?" Howard asked.

"Gosh, you'd be surprised, Agent Watson. The black market has become inundated with sellers of landmines, specifically, anti-personnel landmines. They are simple to make and are cost-effective, which are major factors in explaining their widespread use. I keep finding myself quoting Paul Jefferson, one of the earliest humanitarian deminers, who said, 'A landmine is a perfect soldier; ever courageous, never sleeps, never misses.'"

"Are any of these private military companies in the US? Do we know their names?" Marino asked.

"Yes," she answered. "Several are located in the US. As a matter of fact, located under our feet is one company called Global Tectronics, not exactly a military company, but an IT company headed by a woman named Carla Chaplin and based in Crofton."

"Crofton, Maryland?" Howard asked.

"You seem puzzled by my response, Agent Watson."

"That's because Crofton is what, 30,000 people, and the most news that comes out of that village is whose kid earned the most lucrative college scholarship. Now you're telling us that little Crofton, with its all-too-perfect behavior and its ever-increasing manicured lawns, has been doing big business under our ever-watchful eyes?"

"That's what I'm telling you."

***

Once Callahan left his office, Marino stared at Howard for a lengthy time. Too lengthy, as Howard had to snap his fingers to bring him back to the surface.

"What are you thinking Al," he asked hoping for a really simple "nothing."

"I'm just wondering where Mr. Boris Ramashka lives."

PART TWO

Crofton, Maryland

Boris Ramashka had ordered his lunch at the small but busy restaurant when a headline in the newspaper he was reading caught his eye.

Man's body found in the Chesapeake Bay identified

He dialed a number on his cellphone.

"Meet me at Sunrise Cafe," he said before hanging up.

He continued reading the article. After he finished, he sat back in his seat and was shortly brought out of his oblivion by his waiter delivering his meal.

Fifteen minutes later, a middle-aged Caucasian woman eased herself into his booth.

"What's this about, Bobo?" she asked as she straightened her suit from scooting into the booth.

"Did you see this?" He handed her the newspaper.

"Yes, we saw it, and don't worry," she whispered. "No one will connect that scientist's death with us."

"What do you mean 'us,' Carla?" he whispered back. "I had nothing to do with the kidnapping or death of that man."

Their conversation ceased when the waiter returned and she ordered iced tea.

"Bobo, if you recall, and I certainly hope you do, you were the one who needed that patent. You were the one who told Seffy's people where to find the people developing it." She abruptly quieted and thanked the waiter who brought her tea. "We didn't anticipate that they wouldn't cooperate, but we can't undo that now. The fact that we haven't found the woman yet, or her body, should be more of a concern than that man's death."

32

***

Howard was quite surprised when Agent Callahan called and invited just him to dinner. He kindly turned down the invitation citing some previous engagement but was startled by the woman's confidence. Or was he misreading something into the invitation?

His cousin Carrie told him, "No, Howard, she's smitten. Try not to be alone with her if you can."

Howard smiled to himself. He couldn't remember the last time a woman, besides his wife, actually noticed him. He thought maybe he *was* all that!

Then he looked in the mirror and realized maybe he was just close enough. He couldn't wait to see the grin on Tim's face.

***

Millhouse met Howard at a small cafe in a strip mall in Crofton. Callahan was running late but would meet them later.

"Agent Millhouse…" Howard began.

"Please just call me Millhouse. Gerry and others call me Terrence, but I prefer Millhouse. Is that okay with you, Agent…"

"Call me Howard. And yes, it's fine with me. Actually, I like the sound of your last name. Almost as good as mine."

Both men chuckled.

"Seems you graduated Quantico with one of my men," Howard continued. "Brett Hamilton. How did that go?"

"Brett and I have been friends a long time, maybe not since New Agents Class but certainly when we reported to Phoenix for three years. Then he was transferred, several places, but we kept in touch. But now I see that he's done all right for himself, ending up in your fine unit."

"Yeah, we got lucky. Brett's a great addition to our team. When did you get promoted?"

"A little over six months ago," Millhouse answered. "I'm still trying to process being a Supervisory Special Agent. Although, Gerry is a terrific boss. I now know you, so I'm probably going to be all right."

They clicked their iced tea glasses together.

***

Callahan arrived just when both men thought she wasn't coming. Three glasses of iced tea were enough for both. Howard quickly introduced Millhouse to Callahan.

"Sorry, guys, got caught up in the hoopla of irrelevancy," she said, tossing her red pony tail. "How much did I miss?"

"Not too much," Howard declared. "We're about to drive by Global Tectronics. Wanna join us?"

All three rode in Howard's car, with Millhouse sitting in the front passenger street. Callahan brought along her trusty Nikon camera with the zoom lens…just in case.

The eight-foot-high semi-circular red brick wall with the word CROFTON displayed across it in white letters invited them into the village. Four-story townhouses were all neatly displayed along a circular drive. Huge single-family houses looked as if they could house two or three families in each one. After passing the Crofton Country Club, they spotted the Global Tectronics building, set back from the tree-lined street into a park-like setting. The ten-story, black steel building with green windows seemed to extend the neighborhood's charm.

All three agents simultaneously glanced at their watches when they noticed numerous men and women leaving the main entrance and heading toward their cars.

"Looks like the day shift is over," Millhouse asserted. "What's the woman's name again who heads this up?" He asked.

"Carla Chaplin," Callahan answered. "She's quite astute. Has an interesting background coming out of Johns

Hopkins grad school with an economics degree. She then worked for a high-tech company in Michigan for ten years, moved to France where she worked in banking for about ten years, and then moved back here to Maryland five years ago where she became president of Global Tectronics."

"Why do you know so much about her?" Millhouse asked.

Before Callahan could answer, the focus was on a handsome Black man leaving Global Tectronics and walking to a car.

"Folks, three o'clock," Millhouse said, creating a halt to the conversation. "Andrew Sweeten. What is he doing here? Heading toward a silver-blue Benz."

Before getting in the car, Sweeten leaned against the driver's door, looked around, and dialed a number on his cellphone.

"Who is he, Millhouse?" Howard asked.

"A Person of Interest in backdoor mischief. Got out of Colorado Super Max three months ago."

"Take pictures, Callahan," Millhouse barked. "Zoom in on the number he's dialing."

"His phone's not facing this way, but I can read his lips. He is talking to… Seffy? 'How long should I wait before we know if she is alive. Yeah. Talk soon.'"

Howard and Millhouse turned around in their seats and stared at Callahan.

"What else can you do, Callahan?" Millhouse asked.

***

Sandra Callahan's paternal great-grandfather Flynn emigrated to the US in 1895 in the post-famine era of Irish immigration. He was only fifteen but ready to work, which he did not find for a while due to his red hair, which indicated he was Irish…which meant no job. Many people at this juncture in US history with their limited knowledge of anyone outside themselves, thought the Irish were lazy and foul-smelling because it was believed they didn't bathe.

Callahan was made aware almost immediately after landing in Maryland to beware of the Negroes who were out for his job. Almost instantly, he hated the Negroes as much as he was told they hated him. When he finally got a job as a sweeper on the Baltimore docks, he found out he had to share it with another boy his age…a Negro boy.

The surprise of his life came when he caught the boy reading during his lunch break, something Callahan had yet to learn to do. Immediately the boy put away his book, *Tom Sawyer*, and dropped it into his lunch bucket. Callahan could not believe that this boy not only knew how to read but kept this secret to himself.

Callahan told the boy if he didn't teach him how to read, he would tell others his secret. So three to four evenings each week after work for nearly a year, the two would spend an hour together, and Callahan would not only learn to read but also learn about a different type of courage and perseverance from this boy whose dream was to go to college.

They became lifelong friends, and Flynn Callahan didn't care who knew it.

Flynn Callahan's great-granddaughter Sandra would know courage and perseverance passed down from him and apply it to her life in many ways.

***

Billy Savoy stepped outside the longhouse to converse with the several male elders who were standing in a circle. He waited for his grandfather to get out of his car and walk to the group before starting the meeting.

"You recall us telling you that a man washed up at the lighthouse a couple of days ago when Grandfather and I were fishing?" he asked those gathered.

The men nodded.

"Well, what we didn't mention is he had tape on his mouth, and his hands had been tied behind him just like the woman in the house. There was no identification on him either, and he wore an identical necklace with a small key. I'd say these two people were running from the same enemy."

An elder spoke.

"I think we should find out all we can about these two people to see if *they* are our enemy or an enemy of our enemy."

All the men nodded.

"But the woman doesn't know who she is," Billy remarked. "Don't you think she needs medical help beyond our hands at this time?"

Another elder spoke.

"We do not want strangers upsetting our women and children, Billy, especially if this woman brings unnecessary law enforcement to our village."

All the elders murmured in agreement.

"I believe this woman to be a good soul," Billy's

grandfather said. "She needs our help."

Everyone watched him as he turned and walked slowly to the longhouse.

Another elder spoke.

"Until it is found to be a foolish act, I agree."

***

The middle-aged, slightly portly man walked into Howard's office, not smiling. Howard motioned to him to take a seat at his small conference table.

Howard joined him at the table. "My assistant said you have information about Dr. Serrano that might prove helpful to us. How can we help you, Mr. Glass?" he asked.

"Doctor Steven Glass. I am…was Antony Serrano's husband-to-be," he said, almost choking.

Howard immediately went to his mini-fridge and retrieved bottled water for the man.

"Dr. Glass, I am so sorry for your loss. I was told you were to be married next month?"

"Yes, we were. I am here because I recall something Tony told me, but I filed it away as nonsense."

"Take your time, Dr. Glass."

"We were looking for a cabin several months ago near the Lower Patuxent River area of the Chesapeake for our wedding site. Somehow we got lost but came across a lovely, what we thought was an abandoned, cabin and drove onto the property. No one was around, no cars, no any kind of vehicle. We just wanted to peek in but the door, strangely enough, wasn't locked. It was an office furnished with four desks and computers. We believed we had accidentally trespassed on a company's property, where, you know, they had employee retreats?"

Howard nodded.

"We were on our way out the door when Tony saw a manila folder on a desk labeled *Sensitive*, and of course, he looked in it. The file contained information on landmine patents. What were the odds? Tony thought another company might be competing with his and Paula's invention, so we hurried out. It took us a while to find the main road, but when we did, a large black SUV passed us, going rather fast in the opposite direction. We thought they might be the employees returning."

"Anything else?"

The man became somber.

"I know you're busy with other cases, Agent Watson, but you have to know Tony was the sweetest, kindest person I knew. He was very smart but never made you feel less smart. I loved him. I loved his dry humor and his amazing culinary skills. He meant a lot to me and my life, and I don't know if I'll ever be able to get over his death and how he died. Please don't let his death go by the wayside. Please remember him as a person and not a file number."

"You have my word, Dr. Glass."

The man was almost out the door when he stopped and turned around. "One last thing, Agent Watson. Two weeks ago, Tony thought a car was following him on his way home from work in two different instances. But in both instances, he didn't see the car when he pulled into our driveway."

"Did he say what kind of car?"

"He said a silverish-blue Mercedes."

***

When Howard reported Steven Glass's observations at the cabin, Marino wanted Howard's people to find the place immediately. The problem was Glass could only remember the main highway they took, but not the off-road because he and Dr. Serrano were lost when they stumbled upon the cabin. Howard then called Jim Stanley, who was much more able to assess Maryland's geography.

"Based on what your Dr. Glass described, Howard," Stanley said over the speakerphone, "there are more than two dozen cabins in that river basin that companies use for their employee retreats. I'll send over a map with all of those cabins highlighted for you, and your people can check them out. Another thing, Piscataway Indian land is in that area. Although two Indians reported Dr. Serrano's body hanging on that lighthouse, they won't volunteer to be of any further help. Trust me."

Before hanging up, Howard said, "Jim, you're the best. I owe you dinner."

"Can I pick the place?" Stanley said, chuckling.

***

After receiving the map via messenger, Howard called Tim into his office to discuss the plan of action. He spread the map on his desk.

"This is the general area map in which Dr. Glass believes he and Dr. Serrano were lost. Have Kevin search this area for the cabin Dr. Glass described. Remember, the cabin has a black brick, two-story fireplace located on the outside of the front of the building, and a black door located on the side of the building. Kevin has a lot of geography to cover, but I'm betting that our Dr. Serrano might have been fleeing this cabin."

"What about Dr. Malloy, Howard? Could she be somewhere in or even near that cabin?"

"Good question, Tim. Maybe we should send Brett with Kevin."

***

When Billy walked into the longhouse, his grandfather was holding the young woman's hand.

He turned to Billy and whispered in his ear. "She is a tortured soul right now. She can't remember who she is because those she was fleeing scared her spirit from her soul. We must get her back into her soul."

"Grandfather, I will do what I can to find out who she is…you and Grandmother keep her safe."

Several seconds later an elderly woman stepped forward with a cup of soup. The young woman sat up and drank from the cup.

She beamed at Billy. He beamed back.

"How are you doing this afternoon?" he asked her.

"I believe I'm fine, especially with the wonderful care your grandparents are providing me. Have you found out who I am yet? I need to know. Maybe my parents or husband or children are looking for me. Maybe they think I'm dead!"

The grandmother rubbed her hands. "Billy is looking every day for you, dear. Do not for one moment believe he is not."

***

Billy strolled into the massive Eisenhower Library at Johns Hopkins University in Baltimore and went straight to the free public-access computers. Although he was a Ph.D. candidate at Purdue University in Indiana, he had loved this library since his undergraduate days because it gave him not only a silent place to read and write but a sense of belonging.

In less than six months, his Ph.D. in Agricultural Economics would help him tackle issues related to the production, marketing, distribution, and consumption of food and supporting natural ecosystems. He and the other young people in the settlement felt it was time for their people to provide for their wealth, not from a casino or a handout from the US Government, but a farming concern, generating wealth from their land. Although he had only just turned twenty-seven, the Village Elders appointed him to direct this operation.

After reading through several online newspapers, Billy finally found what he was looking for: *Man's body found in the Chesapeake Bay identified.*

A body found by fishermen that washed up on a lighthouse in the Chesapeake Waterway has been identified as that of a fifty-three-year-old scientist who went missing four days ago. Maryland State Police said the body is that of Dr. Antony Serrano of Arlington, Virginia, and that his body was positively identified through fingerprints. An autopsy was performed and Serrano's cause and manner of death were pending.

Billy looked through several more newspapers but did

not find, almost to his relief, any mention of the woman lying on his grandparents' sofa. As he walked out of the library, an Indian friend was walking in. They both stopped to chat.

"Billy, it's good to see you," the man said while smiling broadly.

"You too, Marty," Billy replied. "What's it been…four, five years?"

"Four for sure; what are you up to these days? Got that Ph.D. yet?"

Billy smiled broadly. "The doctoral hooding ceremony takes place in five months. What have you been up to?"

"I'm still working on my thesis for researching tribal languages and studies, specifically Ojibwa. Unfortunately, a friend who had been helping me for the past year died eight days ago. So, I'm probably looking at graduating next year."

"What a bummer about your friend. Was he sick?"

"*She* drowned, or so I heard. We were becoming good friends, so I found it strange that her family didn't have a funeral for her, especially since I thought Black people believed in funerals. Anyway, it was sad news."

He pointed to his several books in his arms. "I have to hit these books even harder because I'm now on my own with translations unless you know someone who can help me memorize Ojibwa?"

"Sorry, Marty, I wish I had time to help, but it's hard enough keeping up with my grandparents and their old ways."

"This is a paying gig, Billy," Marty said. "They don't have to know Ojibwa—just help me memorize it."

"You know, I do know several young people looking for some income this summer. I'll send them your way. Let me have your digits."

After both men swapped each other's personal information, they said good bye. Before he got to his truck, Billy stopped mid-stream in his tracks and looked back in the direction of his friend, but Marty was nowhere in sight. Something struck Billy as intriguing about the conversation, but he couldn't discern which part. He then got in his vehicle and drove home.

***

Patuxent River Basin

Bounded by the Chesapeake Bay on the east and the Patuxent River on the west, steep cliffs and woods predominate the bay side while along the Patuxent, rolling fields slip gently down to the river. Numerous cabins dotted along this area enjoy the most unbelievable views of the Patuxent.

However wonderful the view, Brett Hamilton and Kevin Lee each said "screw the view" as they were exhausted and wanted to call it quits after four hours in the car. They had traveled over seventy miles, checking out more than twenty cabins, but they had not gotten lucky finding the right cabin. The dark, threatening clouds made it impossible for them to continue. Kevin was driving, so Brett made the call to Tim.

"The closest we got to a cabin that fits somewhat the description Dr. Glass described only had a black door, and no sign of a black fireplace or an office setup," he said. "Seems most of these cabins have red brick fireplaces. We still have about ten to fifteen more cabins to check out but it's getting ready to rain."

"Okay," Tim stated. "Why don't you guys head back and scour the geography again tomorrow? You do know your way back to DC? Right?" Tim chuckled.

Both agents laughed, but not for long.

"Why don't we hit that steakhouse we saw on our way?" Kevin asked.

"Sounds good to me," Brett answered. "Maybe we'll beat what looks like the beginnings of a downpour."

***

Grace Westwood shifted her body in the uncomfortable chair facing John Fleischman's massive desk. She had requested an audience with him for any update on her sister's disappearance. Fleischman read the document to her because he hadn't read it beforehand. She bit her lower lip because she balanced between choking him to death or grabbing the paper out of his hand to read it herself—a hard decision. Luckily for Fleischman, Al Marino walked into his office.

"Major General," Marino began, "I hope you're doing as well as possible under these distressing circumstances."

"Thank you for your concern. Director Fleischman was going over the latest update on the possible whereabouts of Paula. I'm wondering if your people have anything to add to this update at this time?"

Marino looked at Fleischman, who gave him the "go ahead" sign to continue the matter. Marino took the empty chair next to hers.

"I'm afraid nothing concrete, but we're working on several leads surrounding Dr. Serrano's death. We're hoping this information might steer us in the direction of Dr. Malloy's whereabouts and where we'll find her alive."

"I want to thank you, Chief Marino. I've been in this similar situation more times than I can count, delivering the worst news ever about the death of a military loved one. I was under a false impression that I could handle this, but not knowing if my little sister is alive or not has hit me, my brother, and especially my parents, pretty hard."

She paused and took a minute to compose herself.

"Please remember," Marino continued, "our team is working nonstop to get you your answers and offering prayers that will include delivering your sister to you. I do have to ask, did your sister ever mention anything to you or your family regarding anything out of the ordinary, like strange emails or phone calls received that she couldn't explain?"

Westwood took a moment before answering. "No, not really. The only thing I can think of, and this is digging, is that Paula said she was leaving one evening from work and walking toward the train, less than a block away when a young man asked if she needed a ride. My little sister is a good-looking woman, so this invitation was ordinary for her. She told me she wanted to say yes because he was handsome and was driving a Mercedes, but she would never say yes to a stranger, regardless of the car. She said she saw him again two days later parked near the train, but he didn't seem to remember her. She thought she had hurt his feelings."

"Thank you for that information, Major General."

"If you hear of anything," she said to Marino, almost whispering, "any little thing, anything of any obscure nature, would you let me know?"

"Of course we will," Fleischman announced.

Marino walked her to the door.

***

All Howard could do was shake his head.

"I mean, what does John do up there on the sixth floor?" he asked Marino.

Marino chuckled. "You know as well as I do that we work around him. That's been part of our saving grace. Sure, he'll take credit for this case once we solve it, but it could be worse. He could be going through our files and trying to figure out how'this stuff works."

Both men laughed.

Marino's assistant announced Tim's arrival via his speakerphone. He looked at Howard quizzically.

"He's got an update on this case," Howard revealed, "and I thought we should hear it together."

Tim took a seat at Marino's table. "Good morning Chief, Howard."

Both nodded.

"Ahmad has come up with a rather interesting idea after visiting with those analysts. He figured if we're going after Ramashka and others, perhaps we could school *him* on landmines and present him as a seller of an invention also focusing on detection, just like Serrano and Malloy. What do you think?"

"Sounds plausible, but how would Ahmad be able to pull in Ramashka?" Howard asked.

"That's what he needs to work on, but you know Ahmad, all he has to do is invent it."

"Yes, we know Waverly." Marino smirked. "What do you think, Howard?"

"I think it will be tricky and maybe even expensive to

set up, but if you, Director, say it's a 'go,' then we're in."

Marino shook his head slowly. "Now, all I have to do is sell the idea to John. I need details, details, details. And I need them today."

***

In the basement of the 1.5 million square foot Global Tectronics building, twenty people were processing 32-bit microcontrollers for development boards going to the Central African Republic. These particular warehouse people only worked at night.

Carla Chaplin was the captain of this tremendous undertaking that made her very cushy life possible and hugely successful for her shareholders who had no idea of how the company's hardware and machinery were being used.

Chaplin was originally from Maryland but moved to Michigan for ten years with an IT company and then across the water to France to take a position in banking. She met Seffy Mischicot shortly after his return to France after graduate school in the United States. After being introduced to the young Mischicot, she became immediately enamored, but he only saw her as an invaluable arm to his grandfather…nothing else. She recognized he was ten years her junior, but as bright as she thought of herself, she never realized he saw nothing in her except that she was brilliant.

Chaplin reported to Mischicot's grandfather in the foreign exchange division of their headquarters in the "pink city" of Toulouse. Within two years of appointment, she was promoted to Foreign Exchange Director because of her economics background, fluency in French, and serving their American ex-pat community well. She loved everything about France, its food, wine region, and language.

She worked for the Mischicot family organization for ten years when their company in the US, Global Tectronics, was jolted by the news of the sudden death of the President/CEO. They had to scramble to find a new one. After nearly two months of the company saying no to various applicants for various reasons, Chaplin applied for the job and was shocked when she landed the position. Without further ado, she moved back to the states, especially after recognizing that Mischicot couldn't give a rat's ass about her.

After a successful year at the helm in Maryland, Seffy stepped back into Chaplin's life when he flew to the US and introduced her to a friend...Boris Ramashka. Both Mischicot and Ramashka wined and dined her for several days before finally telling her about their lucrative mission in black market landmines. *Did she want in?*

Chaplin was highly disappointed in the so-called courtship because she thought Mischicot had flown to the US to see her but quickly realized he needed her, not wanted her. *Miscalculation again;* she couldn't help herself. She decided, at least with this venture, she would be around him, regardless of how he felt about her. Once she became fully aware that Ramashka and Mischicot liked each other way more than Seffy could ever like her, Chaplin settled into the "third wheel" part of their relationship, where she felt safe...but invisible.

***

Brett and Kevin set off for lands unknown again as they scoured the Patuxent River basin, searching for the ever-elusive cabin. Two hours into the field trip, they found it. This time Brett was driving.

"I think we found the place, Tim," Kevin said over the speaker of his cellphone.

"Turn on your camera so that I can see what we're talking about," Tim replied.

"Yep, that's it, guys," Tim announced.

After noticing no vehicles on the property and no sign of human action coming from the cabin, Brett and Kevin got out of their car. They walked carefully toward the house while Kevin kept the camera on the place, and Brett removed his gun from its holster. They strolled up to the black door on the side of the cabin. It was locked. Both men peered into the window. No movement inside and no visible signs of anyone at the house; also no desks and no computers.

"What do you want us to do, Tim?" Brett asked.

"Don't break anything trying to get inside. Take me off-camera, and later let me know what you find inside."

***

Howard and Tim were disappointed that Brett and Kevin found nothing like what Dr. Glass had described. The cabin looked as if no one had been there for weeks. It had been thoroughly cleaned. Howard wanted to know why.

"Tim," he said, looking perplexed, "send Brett and Kevin back to the area again. I want them to scour the outside perimeter of that cabin, looking for trash, wires, papers, anything that signals someone had been there in the past two weeks. Dr. Glass described the cabin to a T. I'm convinced that that was the cabin. But why is it now empty?"

***

The young woman didn't know why but she felt safe with these people and the elderly couple taking care of her. She felt incredibly safe with the young man named Billy. But she needed to know who *she* was. Why was she wearing a necklace with a key? What did the key open? Had she done something terrible?

Billy was pulling up in his truck outside the longhouse when he saw his grandmother rocking slowly on the porch with what he deemed an alarmed look on her face.

"What is it, Grandmother? What's wrong?" he asked as he was sliding out of his truck.

"She had a nightmare, Billy. She was yelling, 'Don't hit him again! Don't hit him again!' It was in an evil dream!"

***

Boris Ramashka lived in the gated part of the neighborhood in Crofton where the district paid the guards well. No one entered unless an owner told the guards to expect their visitor. No one entered or exited without the guards taking driver licenses or identification.

When Howard and Millhouse presented their FBI credentials and the guards were told not to announce their presence to anyone, the guards did not know how to handle this type of proceeding. Sure, they'd had the police before for some loud party that didn't know how to end, but never the FBI. Never.

As the agents drove along the winding streets, the houses seemed to get larger the more they ventured into the enclave of manicured lawns. When they reached Ramashka's house, an older man in overalls was treating his lawn. Howard and Millhouse drove past slowly, parking down the street. The house was attractive but not spectacular, especially for someone raking in millions of dollars generated from lucrative landmine sales.

"I guess this is how he's been able to stay under the radar," Millhouse noted. "Nothing too ostentatious. Nothing too blatant."

Howard looked at him. "Ostentatious?"

"Yeah," Millhouse answered. "A word the always-present teachers in my family use."

Both men laughed until they noticed a silver-blue Mercedes pull up in front of Ramashka's house.

"Well, look what we have here," Millhouse announced. "Andrew Sweeten. He must be on the visitor's list since the guards let him through."

"Let's see how long he stays," Howard said.

It seemed a long thirty minutes but Sweeten finally left Ramashka's house. The wait paid off as the perk was that Ramashka walked him to his car. They continued a few minutes of talk before Sweeten got in his Mercedes and drove off. Ramashka said a few words to the gardener and then went back inside his house.

"So we now have proof," Howard declared, "that Sweeten and Ramashka know each other. I wonder what they were saying? Too bad Callahan isn't here when we need her."

***

Kevin and Brett returned to the cabin to look for whatever Howard believed they missed the first time. They had been searching diligently through weeds, bushes, and trash when they stumbled on a circle of rocks used for a fire pit located 100 feet from the cabin. Kevin saw what looked like remnants of burnt papers, and when both men searched more closely, two words appeared on what they deemed were originally driver licenses.

"Yes, Tim," Brett said over the speaker on his cellphone. "The name Paula was still clear enough for us to make out on one license and the letters s-e-r on the other license. Amazingly, these were still in that pit because it rained."

"We got lucky," Tim said. "But now we know Malloy and Serrano were at that cabin. Bring back all remnants if you can. If you can't, make sure you take all the pictures. See you soon."

Once they returned to the main road, a black SUV passed them, traveling in the opposite direction.

"Do you think that was the vehicle Dr. Glass described?" Kevin asked Brett.

Brett pulled over to the side of the road and called Tim.

"By now," Tim said, "you both know how to get to that cabin blindfolded. Take another route, so those in the vehicle don't realize you're following them. Report to me ASAP and wait for any further instructions. Lock and load."

Brett turned the car around and proceeded on another path to the cabin. When they reached an area near the house, both men got out of their vehicle, took two pairs of binoculars from the glove department, and quietly watched the place from behind a shanty fifty yards away.

"We see the cabin, Tim," Brett whispered into the phone, "but no activity."

"Stay close to the action," Tim said, "but don't invite any fire. Understand me?"

Both men clearly understood. Five minutes later, four body-building-looking Black men exited the cabin, looked around the environment, and then got into the black SUV, unknowingly passing by Brett and Kevin. One of the Black men had a dark briefcase in his hands.

"Where did the guy get the briefcase, Brett?" Kevin asked. "We looked everywhere in that cabin for signs of someone having been there, and we didn't see a briefcase."

"Yeah, and he didn't look like the type of guy who carries a briefcase," Brett added.

Afterward, Kevin reported to Tim what they saw and were happy they did not have to confront anyone.

They drove to the cabin and looked throughout the place again but still found no signs of human activity.

As they were leaving, Brett noticed that a section of the paneling seemed very different from the rest of the wall. Both men went over to the area, and Kevin slid his fingers around the section when three panels jutted out of position. Kevin pulled on the slats and was met with a doorknob. Both men looked at each other for a pregnant moment, and then Kevin turned the knob, and the door on the wall opened up to reveal steps going down to what they believed was a cellar.

"Should both of us or one of us go down?" Kevin

asked.

"Since you're already there, you go," Brett answered. "I'll make sure no one sneaks up on us."

Kevin switched on the flashlight part of his cellphone and made his way down the stairs. He looked around the cellar and noticed empty coke and water bottles. He called up to Brett to make sure he was still there.

"I don't see anything unusual down here, Brett. Hold on…"

He was about to walk back up the stairs when he spied something on the floor. Two pairs of eyeglasses.

"These look like male and female glasses. Do you think they might belong to the two doctors? This one has the initials AS inside the frame. It looks like it has blood on it."

"I don't know, Kevin, but let's get them back to the Bureau and have the lab check them out."

They scrambled to their vehicle and headed back to DC.

***

Ahmad had been working diligently with Drs. Tran and Ha on a "dummy" invention for a landmine spotting system when John Fleischman asked for an update on the development.

"What is he looking for, Al?" Howard asked in an almost angry tone.

"Cool it, Howard," Marino answered, shaking his head. "Since John okayed the project, he thinks he has a right to know how it's progressing. I'm in agreement since we're shelling out several thousands of dollars to see this case resolved."

"But, Al, he has no idea what he's looking for, or what he's looking at. What gives?"

"Let's just sit back and relax and watch Ahmad explain the mechanics and the process for which we can move on to the next step: reining in Ramashka, Mischicot, and possibly this Sweeten guy."

***

When Tim and Ahmad entered Marino's office later that afternoon, Fleischman was already seated at Marino's desk…in Marino's chair. Marino and Howard were sitting on the sofa. Tim and Ahmad took seats at Marino's conference table. After being given the "go ahead" sign from Marino, Ahmad produced a black leather bracelet, a miniature drone the size of his hand, and a minuscule disc the size of his thumbnail to show to the group.

"As we all know," he began, "anti-personnel landmines are designed to explode when as little as two kilograms of pressure is applied or when a person steps on them or disturbs them. So, first we release this drone in the area intended. It then connects to this 32-bit wireless microcontroller in this bracelet that someone will be wearing, which will then send a fake signal that pressure is on it to any landmine within twenty feet and it will explode."

"Will this work?" Fleischman asked.

Everyone looked at him in disbelief.

"Director," Ahmad began, "I'm just developing a scenario to be sold to the highest bidder in the room, which hopefully will be Boris Ramashka and his satanic underlings."

Howard and Tim hid their smiles.

"How will Ramashka find out about this?" Fleischman asked.

Tim signaled to Ahmad to have a seat. He then spoke to the gathered. "We plan on hitting the dark web and make Ahmad appear to be a competitor in the race to the patent office. We believe whoever killed Dr. Serrano, and possibly Dr. Malloy, didn't get their invention, so Ahmad might have a chance to pull in the greedy by demonstrating his so-called microchip."

"Microcontroller, Tim," Ahmad whispered.

Tim hid his smile again and continued. "We would set up some type of dummy room and make sure Ahmad's "controller" works in that room. At this time, we're still working on the mechanics."

Everyone rose from their seats when Fleischman rose from Marino's desk.

"Well, when will we be able to see this so-called finished mechanism, Agent Waverly?" Fleischman asked.

"Soon, sir," he answered. "Soon."

"That's not the answer I want to hear, but I understand."

He looked at Marino. "Make sure soon is soon."

Marino nodded.

***

The woman woke up in the middle of the night screaming. Within minutes, Billy's grandfather and grandmother were by her side on the sofa.

"Wake up, my dear, it's just a dream!" the grandmother cried.

"You're hurting him! You're hurting him!" she screamed.

The grandmother went quickly to the cooking area to make some herbal tea. The grandfather took her hands and started rubbing them with lavender oil that he believed would calm her down within a few minutes. Others in the longhouse, also awakened abruptly, gathered at the sofa. They murmured various things among themselves.

"Why are you saying I'm crazy?" she shouted.

The assembled looked at her incredulously. They spoke in an Algonquin language, but how would she know that? At that moment, Billy ran into the house in his pajamas and knelt by her on the sofa. His grandfather told him that she understood the Algonquin language—how was this possible?

"I don't know," she said, shaking her head. "I don't know how I know this."

Billy was intrigued, mostly because she was not an Indian. He then spoke to her in Algonquin but she didn't seem to understand him. His grandmother brought her the tea, which she drank while his grandfather rubbed her neck and shoulders with the lavender oil. She soon returned to sleep.

"Billy," his grandmother said softly. "The people she is screaming about are hurting someone she knows."

"No, Grandmother," he answered slowly. "The people she is screaming about *killed* someone she knows."

One of the elders spoke softly but adamantly. "We think it is time to let her go to her people."

"That will not happen on my watch," Billy declared.

"What Billy say, I say too," his grandmother uttered.

Everyone went slowly back to their beds.

***

It was three a.m., and Howard couldn't sleep. He tossed and turned in the bed too many times until his wife Carol told him to go into his study or watch television. He went into the living room, turned the volume down low, and was treated to a western. He became slightly perturbed by the look of the Indians in the movie, who were white men portrayed with dark makeup. He turned to another channel. Another western perpetuating stereotypes involving Native Americans! He turned to another channel—Davy Crockett!

Howard was about to puke his dinner. Then a lightbulb clicked on.

Wow, why hadn't he thought of this before?

He turned off the television, went into his study, clicked open his computer on the desk, and started making geographical comparisons. Looking at the maps, he commented aloud, "This makes sense. Yeah, this makes sense."

He needed to call Jim Stanley the following day for his opinion.

***

Al Marino was in Gerry Kramer's office in Baltimore when Millhouse and Howard trekked through. They were there to solidify a strategy for arresting Boris Ramashka and the rest of his cronies.

"Al and I believe we've devised a plan for Waverly to exhibit his knowledge of landmines," Kramer said, "and want both of you to approve this stratagem so we can move forward."

Howard and Millhouse each took a couple of minutes to read the draft.

"I like it," Millhouse said after reading the document.

"I agree with Millhouse," Howard announced. "Hopefully we can use your team, Gerry. My people are all on assignment in this case."

"This is okay with me. Al, you okay with this?"

Marino nodded.

"No problem, as John already approved your team in this budget, Gerry."

Marino looked oddly at Howard.

"I'm thinking of taking a trip to Piscataway territory," He said.

"Why?" Marino asked. "What's in Piscataway country?"

"Something is gnawing at me about the two Native Americans who found Dr. Serrano's body and called authorities. Ahmad had a conversation with Dr. Ha about one of Dr. Malloy's friends. Seems Malloy has been helping a Ph.D. candidate with his thesis on tribal languages and studies."

"And?" Marino asked.

"And I talked with Jim Stanley this morning about the distance between where the two Native Americans found Dr. Serrano's body and the actual Piscataway settlement grounds. He said maybe three miles, maybe less."

"What does Dr. Serrano and the Piscataway tribe have in common?"

"Don't know yet. Natives don't try to help us 'foreigners,' but maybe we're talking about a couple of Natives who might know more than they said. Maybe they'll talk to me, maybe not. Anyway, maybe the Native American who Dr. Malloy was helping lives on or near Piscataway land and he'll talk to us."

"Maybe Terrence should accompany you," Kramer said. "He's been on their turf before."

"Yeah, but they didn't seem to like me, if you recall," Millhouse added.

"What about Callahan?" Kramer asked. "She needs something to do."

Howard hid his protest, believing it was too much to explain.

***

With the assistance of the FBI Undercover Sensitive Operations Unit, Ahmad became a bearded, eyeglass-wearing, wig-wearing inventor. In addition, the IT department created an in-depth resume that those on the dark web would have difficulty challenging. Howard and Tim did not know Ahmad when he passed them in the hallway.

"I am impressed," Howard told him. "Wait until Al gets a load of you."

"Give me some credit. In the past twelve years, you guys have seen me in more disguises than I can count on both hands."

***

Marino was impressed; however, he wanted to make sure that Ahmad understood the assignment perfectly and that if he felt something was not at all legitimate, he was to pull out of the mission, pronto. Ahmad was so pumped he could have inflated all the tires on his car with his breath. Of course, Tim felt uneasy about Ahmad being "out there" by himself.

"Give it up, Tim," Ahmad told him. "You sound like my wife, and you look nothing like her. Besides, Millhouse's people will have my back."

"When are we meeting with them?" Tim asked.

"I checked with your secretary so in the morning if that's okay with you?"

Tim nodded in approval.

"Right now though, I'm headed over to IT to peruse my new resume as 'Francis I. Benoit' from Haiti."

"You finally get to use your French," Howard added.

"*Oui et je suis content.*"

"I guess that means you're happy?"

"You know it."

***

Tim and Ahmad met with Millhouse and three of his agents over breakfast the next morning in the small cafe across the street from the four-story FBI Baltimore facility. Ahmad, but mostly Tim, was impressed with the Baltimore team, especially the two agents who previously worked in Quantico's crime labs and the third agent who previously worked on a terrorism task force. Their many questions were music to Tim's ears.

Millhouse laid out a small map of Baltimore on the table after everyone had eaten.

"Waverly, we've set up your meeting at a historical but empty small hotel in the Cherry Hill section of the city. Yeah, we know it's the ghetto, but it also makes sense because you're a person of color so no one will be confused as to why you're there."

Ahmad nodded as Millhouse continued.

"The several risks will include outside violence and the crumbling buildings, so do not stand too close to the old brick buildings and don't walk around at night."

Everyone managed to smile at the joke used to ease tensions.

"Seriously," he continued, "my unit here understands everything about the spotting system you and your team have developed. They will be part of the hotel staff to ensure your rooms, cigars, and beverage needs are satisfied, but there will be no meals. So we're looking at an after-hours type of meeting to go down. The hotel is only open for Francis Benoit's needs, but no one else's because Mr. Benoit is a 'special' client of the owner, who we'll create later."

"This is cool," Ahmad announced.

"Also, Waverly, all three of these guys are fluent in French. We chose them for this purpose."

'C'est genial!' Ahmad shouted.

The Baltimore agents smiled broadly. Tim grinned.

***

Calvert County is nine miles wide at its widest point, boasting some of the best farmland in the state, making farming a laborious initiative but lucrative benefit to all living in the area. Farming dominated the Patuxent's economy for the two centuries following white settlement, with about sixty percent of Maryland's tobacco coming from the Patuxent Valley. Formerly a cash crop in Maryland, tobacco farms were virtually extinct due to the many lawsuit settlements of the tobacco companies. Tobacco farmers sold most of their land to developers and new home buyers.

Billy and others had difficulty convincing some of the elders that they would not get their stolen land back any time soon, so purchasing it made all the sense in the world...just not to them. But this enterprising and innovative band of Piscataway stopped intertribal fighting for over a year, pooled their resources together, and bought as much land as they could afford—1,421 acres, or two and a quarter square miles. It was a beginning.

***

After two weeks, the woman no longer needed help walking, and asked to see the community. Billy mostly drove her around, pointing out the many perks of the area. He was careful about asking her questions to which he believed he knew the answer, but she would not. He also hoped he hadn't tired her out from her first field trip into the woods. He thought she was beautiful and seemed bright from her many questions. He couldn't imagine who could have possibly wanted to hurt her. And why?

He was pretty excited about surrendering his dream to this stranger. However, he wanted her to know that what he was working towards was much more than a farming concern. The farming concern would authorize them to use the land for its intention: to grow food for the care, cultivation, and breeding of crops and animals. He and numerous other young people in the community had been working towards their master's and doctoral degrees in agriculture to manage such a feat within the next two years. The land issue was as important as Billy's unshakeable quest to end the forever fight over "Who is carrying the real bloodline of the Piscataway people? How ludicrous! How insane!"

"I'm working toward a connection," he complained softly to the woman. "I want my people to connect again. We seem to be moving in opposite directions over what? Nothing. Scraps that are thrown at us. Our ancestors are watching. They have to be deeply saddened by what they see."

It looked like rain, so he cut the trip short. After

parking the pickup, they hurried back to the longhouse. Billy placed windbreakers over their heads to protect them from the rain. In the interval, he noticed a dark-colored sedan driving up to the municipal building in the main square. A Black man and a red-haired woman got out of the car.

It was now raining hard.

***

Howard and Callahan glanced around the square but only for a moment as it was starting to rain. A man and a woman ran past their car and headed toward a longhouse. They had their jackets pulled up over their heads. He and Callahan then dashed to the two-story white building that housed the Tribal Police Department, village information, documents, and the US Post Office. Howard secured the attention of the female clerk almost immediately. He and Callahan then displayed their FBI credentials, causing the clerk to become less interested.

"I hope you can help us," he said. "This is a picture of a woman we believe has been kidnapped and is missing. Have you seen this woman?"

The clerk took a few seconds but shook her head no.

"Would you mind displaying this picture on your wall, in case someone *has* seen her?"

The clerk nodded, took the picture from Howard, and stapled it to the bulletin board on the wall.

"Should anyone have any information regarding her whereabouts they can reach me as my name and phone number are on the back. Is there someone we can talk to in the Tribal Police department?"

The clerk pointed to the stairway. "Lieutenant Swann is one flight up."

When Howard and Callahan reached the top of the stairway, a massive clap of thunder rattled the stairs under their feet. A deputy officer pointed to Lieutenant Swann, seated at his desk with a giant bronze desk nameplate that paraded his name and title. He looked up from whatever he was reading and nodded to both people to take a seat. He went back to reading.

"What can we do for you?" he asked without looking up from his newspaper.

Howard and Callahan displayed their FBI credentials.

"As I just said, what can we do for you?"

After explaining the disappearance of both scientists and mentioning that two Piscataway Natives had pulled one of the scientists from the Chesapeake, Howard wondered if he could talk with the Indians who had called the authorities.

"Whew, what a story." Swann whistled. "You can't make this stuff up. If you have a picture of this scientist and we happen to see her, should I give you a call?"

Howard felt this trip was a waste of time, so he nodded to Callahan that it was time to leave. Another giant clap of thunder hit their ears.

"My suggestion to you both," Swann remarked dryly, looking out his window, "is that you should seek cover as soon as you can because it's about to let loose in the sky, and when it rains here, the roads get flooded, and sometimes you can't go nowhere for two-three days."

Before heading down the stairs, Howard gave Swann his card and offered a handshake, but Swann returned to reading his newspaper. Once they departed, Swann glanced over at his deputy, smiled, tore up Howard's card, and threw it in the trash.

Outside, it was pouring. Howard and Callahan dashed to the car, where they sat for almost twenty minutes, trying to ride out the downpour.

***

Finally, the rain had decreased to an almost drizzle, allowing them to safely leave the area. In the less than thirty minutes of rain, flooding had taken hold of the road, but Howard tried successfully for a while at least in maneuvering the sedan so the vehicle wouldn't hydroplane. Except it did, and they became stuck in the mud on the shoulder. Howard removed his jacket and was about to get out of the car when Callahan stopped him.

"Hold up, Agent Watson. First, let *me* get behind the wheel, and you rock the car back and forth. If that doesn't work, let's place the floor mats under the tires. And if that doesn't work, we can try letting a little air out of the tires."

It took more than a minute, but the floor mats helped ease the car out of the mud, but not before the earth became part of Howard's wardrobe, as he was covered in mud. Callahan could not stop laughing. She then slipped and fell while retrieving the mats under the tires. It was then Howard's turn to laugh.

"Agent Watson," she said, pointing. "I'm starving. Why don't we stop at that drive-thru restaurant over there so we won't have to get out of the car?"

Howard had to admit that he was also famished. He then pulled the car over to a dry shoulder, got out, went into his trunk, and retrieved two towels and a shirt. He gave Callahan a towel and the shirt and turned his back as she took off her blazer and blouse and replaced them with the shirt, several sizes too big.

"Callahan, I suppose you can now call me Howard, especially since you're wearing one of my emergency shirts."

"Thanks, Howard. Since we're buddies now, tell me more about your family."

"Not at this time, but if you need to spill the beans about yours, go ahead. I'll pretend to listen."

And spill the beans she did. However, at that point, Howard got a chuckle out of the redhead. More importantly, he was impressed with her clear thinking regarding their car situation and that she had the problem under control from the start. *It must be the fortitude and restraint needed as a bomb tech.*

Once Howard and Callahan left the confines of the Piscataway Nation and had satisfied their stomachs at the nearby "finger-licking good" place, they headed back to DC.

Because Marino had a barrage of questions waiting for him, Howard decided to call it a day. He then dropped off Callahan at her townhouse in DC, where she asked if he wanted to come in and share a drink? He let her down without effort by pointing out how he looked and how he must smell. He then headed home to Virginia.

He would deal with everything the next day.

***

Marino's questions were many. Howard's answers were few but still seemed to satisfy Marino.

"Why did you believe the Indians were going to speak with you…because you had a woman with you?" Marino asked without batting an eye.

"No," Howard answered, shaking his head. "I was going to go to the place myself until Kramer volunteered Callahan."

He then chuckled.

"However, had it not been for Callahan, we would probably still be on Indian land stuck in the mud up to our knees."

Marino went into his desk and retrieved a cigar that he ran across his nose. He then got up from his desk and stood in front of his picture window that faced the Washington Mall. The soft patter of the rain possibly caused him to linger longer than he wanted.

"Where is that scientist?" he asked without turning around. "It's been two weeks. Why haven't we found her or her body like Dr. Serrano?"

"I don't know, Al," Howard said, shaking his head. "Maybe she's not dead but being held somewhere or hiding somewhere?"

"If she's hiding somewhere, you'd think she would be able to contact someone who could help her."

"Maybe she's hurt."

"Maybe. How is Waverly coming along with his resume on the dark web, as you call it?" he asked, still staring out at the rain.

"As soon as you enter the name Francis I. Benoit or his prototype, a flag will send that person to our clandestine site. Mounds of information anywhere from the development of other patents to career and education resumes are listed on our Haitian."

"Sounds good. How will this meeting take place?"

"As of now, the requestor goes to a link, then a flag then waves on our site, and Mr. Benoit will set up the meeting. By the way, Ahmad says Benoit's initials are FIB."

"Cute. John wants an update tomorrow afternoon, especially since Waverly is up and running. I want you all in my office tomorrow morning."

***

Townhouse in Baltimore

After passing a high-end shopping mall and several small boutiques, the gorgeous-looking three-story townhouse was almost a letdown inside as it had all the charm of a museum. Of course the owner was worldly. All kinds of art, artifacts, and sculptures were visible throughout, but the place seemed void of life. The location was expensive, too, as the Smithsonian and other historical monuments were less than twenty minutes away.

Carla Chaplin was sitting on a leather barstool in her high-end stainless steel kitchen talking on her phone.

"No, Seffy, we haven't found her or her body yet," she said. "Okay, I'll pick you up at Dulles in the morning. Yes, Bobo will be there. Why do we have to have to include Sweeten? He'll just screw shit up again. Okay, okay, we'll all connect tomorrow evening. Yes, we have the meeting with that Haitian scheduled for Friday night. See you tomorrow."

When she hung up with Mischicot, Chaplin wondered how deeper the situation would get if the woman scientist were found alive. They had to find her, she thought. *We have to find her.*

She then placed her two calls to Ramashka and Andrew Sweeten.

***

She arrived later at Ramashka's house in the pouring rain. Andrew Sweeten, her irritation of the month, appeared a few minutes later. They each tried coming up with a strategy to bilk the Haitian out of his invention for over an hour. None of their suggestions seemed to make sense. After researching Benoit thoroughly and his several copyrights, they believed they had found another guinea pig who was racing to the patent office. If they could buy his invention, their lucrative landmine stockpiling business would remain intact. They didn't want to think about another person who would be saying no to their offer. But just in case, they also filed away the fact that Benoit's parents were dead; he was a single male with no children or siblings.

"What if this Francis guy doesn't want to sell?" Sweeten asked.

"First of all, his name is Benoit," Chaplin pointed out. "Secondly, Seffy would have to take care of this as you have already fucked up our other situation."

"What the hell are you talking about?" he yelled at her.

Ramashka gave a heavy sigh.

"Why do I have to keep separating you two? All of us are in this shit together, whether we like it or not. And like Seffy says, if we don't find that woman scientist or hope she's dead, we all go to prison for a lengthy time."

"I ain't going back to prison," Sweeten said as he rummaged through Ramashka's refrigerator.

"Well, it's been two weeks," Chaplin countered, "and her body hasn't floated to any surface nor found on the ground, so I believe she's alive and in hiding."

"If she's in hiding, wouldn't she contact the law?" Ramashka asked.

"Don't know," she answered. "Maybe the Injuns got her."

All three laughed.

***

Billy Savoy could not shake the something on his mind.

He looked up his friend Marty's number and called him. He got his voicemail. He would wait for Marty to return his call.

After waiting almost half a day, Marty finally returned Billy's call.

"Man, Billy," he said. "Didn't realize I left my phone and my wallet in my car because I usually don't take my phone with me while I'm teaching. But I needed my wallet to eat. Sorry, I'm just getting back to you. Got some income 'needers' for me?"

"Not at this time, Marty, although I put the word out. I'm calling because I want to ask the name of your friend who was helping you with your Ojibwa, and she drowned."

"Oh, her name was Paula Malloy. She was a scientist working in an Army lab in Baltimore on some 'secret mission,' she called it. Smart woman and pretty nice looking too."

"So, she would have picked up some Algonquin that is closely related to Ojibwa if she helped you memorize for almost a year, right?"

"Uh, yeah, Billy. Where are we going with this?"

"Marty, I need your help. I need you to come to the nation and possibly identify this woman we found unconscious in Cat Hole Trail about three weeks ago. She doesn't know who she is and we think she has amnesia. But, if she is Paula Malloy, people are trying to kill her."

"What?" he shouted on the phone. "What?"

"Marty, can I count on you not to mention this to anyone and just get here as soon as possible?"

"Hell, yeah, Billy, I'll be there in the morning."

***

Grace Westwood and Steven Glass were called individually to Marino's office to identify the eyeglasses found at the cabin in Maryland. Steven Glass broke down when he recognized Dr. Serrano's glasses. The initials AS in gold etching inside the frame solidified the identification. Hours later, Grace Westwood identified Paula Malloy's eyeglasses.

"Please understand," Marino said to her, "we have no evidence that she is not alive. We are still looking. You must trust us in this process."

Westwood left the office clinging to her little sister's glasses at her breast.

***

Howard met Marino in his office earlier than he wanted to meet with him. After sifting through the doughnuts Marino bought and pouring himself some coffee, Howard learned that Francis Benoit received a hit on the link of the covert website regarding a party who would be interested in buying or buying in on his spotting system invention. The party left a direct message mailbox. Ahmad had answered the message and said he would be interested in talking with the party but wanted to know how the party knew he had an invention for a spotting system?

As Howard and Marino each read the complete message, Marino felt almost naive, not knowing that so much illegality was happening on the world wide web, and he wouldn't know where to start to reign in just a tiny percentage of it.

"You know, I was just thinking, Al," Howard remarked. "We should use Callahan as the owner of that hotel. She's fluent in French, has a bold personality, and doesn't rattle easily."

"I don't know," Marino replied. "How would we use her, besides being the hotel owner?"

"Remember, Benoit is one of her 'personal' clients, so she would want to be where he is, which means making sure staff is making the drinks, handling the cigars, freshening up the rooms, speaking in French, staying in their lane, and don't forget, she can read lips from a distance."

"So we're putting another agent in harm's way? I know she's a bomb tech, but does Callahan even know how to handle a weapon?"

"She told me she's an excellent shot. As long as Millhouse's guys have Ahmad's back, she'll be fine."

"Where are your people?" Marino barked. "I said a nine A-M meeting."

"Al, it's eight thirty."

Not ten minutes later, Tim, Ahmad, Brett, Kevin, Millhouse, and Callahan breezed through his door. Howard then directed the group into Marino's adjacent conference room.

"This is where we are right now," Howard began. "First, Dr. Malloy's body has not materialized and Al and I believe that she's alive and in hiding."

"If she's in hiding," Tim asked, "why hasn't she contacted authorities?"

"Don't know that answer, Tim, unless she doesn't trust anyone."

"Well, if she *is* alive," Callahan countered, "someone must be feeding her."

All eyes looked at Callahan.

"What? What did I say?" she asked.

"You might be right," Howard declared. "It's been almost three weeks. She would have starved by now. She's staying somewhere, maybe in one of those cabins, especially the corporate ones where there's always canned and packaged food."

"Yes," Tim added, "and when guests look like they're arriving, she moves on to another cabin."

Marino shook his head slowly. "That's a lot of guessing, folks. It could be simple. She could be dead."

The room went quiet.

"Okay, Waverly, you're up," Marino said.

Ahmad displayed four devices to the group: a round, rubbery black disc that would fit in a person's palm; a drone the size of a person's hand; a black leather bracelet; and finally, a square microcontroller disc the size of a thumbnail. First, because the chain was rather small, he asked Callahan to place the bracelet on her ankle. He then requested Millhouse to hold the rubbery round disc in his hand, put the drone on the disc, and move to the opposite end of the conference room, far away from the door. Ahmad then set a small covered box with four oranges in the middle of the floor.

"Callahan, walk outside and close the door."

"I'm not gonna die, am I, Waverly?"

"Uh, not right now."

She walked outside the conference room door.

"Callahan, close the door."

"Millhouse, after you turn on the red button on the drone, keep your hand open with the disc on it."

The drone left the rubbery disc, and Millhouse's hand, hovered over the small box on the floor for thirty-seconds, and then went back to Millhouse's hand.

"Ohhhkaaaay." Marino said slightly unimpressed.

"I'm not done," Ahmad announced. "Callahan, come back in!"

She walked back into the room, and Ahmad asked her to place the microcontroller disc in the slit of the ankle bracelet and leave the room again. After she left the room, Ahmad asked Millhouse to once again turn on the red button on the drone. This time the drone hovered over the box for less than thirty-seconds, sent a laser beam to the box, and the box blew up and the oranges were sent flying. The drone then returned to Millhouse's hand.

The entire group went crazy.

"This is amazing, Waverly," Marino said, trying not to smile. "How did it work?"

"Well, the drone's getting a signal from the microcontroller in Callahan's…get Callahan back in here!"

Callahan strolled back into the room and wondered what had happened to make everyone in the room seem so awake.

"I'll explain it again," Ahmad said. "According to Drs. Tran and Ha, Serrano and Malloy were working on a drone that would send a fake signal to a landmine, and the landmine, believing weight was on it, would blow up. Now the microchip that the scientists designed on a way larger and more complex scale, different from mine, involved interaction with a drone. The drone and microcontroller work in tandem with each other. Because the drone is small, it can hover undetected over the intended area. The ankle bracelet with the disc inside, if within twenty feet of a landmine, would signal the drone to destroy it."

The applause was welcomed.

"Last thing," Ahmad divulged, "this device will last for only three operations because the batteries in the drone and bracelet are just store-bought lithium batteries, and I wouldn't want our buyers to think they could just go out and make this themselves…without me."

Later that afternoon, in Fleischman's conference room, Kramer et al. were in awe of Ahmad's invention. Tim and Howard could be no prouder of him than his wife, who expected a significant bonus in his next paycheck.

***

Mischicot stepped out of the airport terminal and immediately saw Chaplin waving to him from across three lanes of arrival traffic.

"Where's Bobo?" he asked almost immediately.

"He's at home preparing your welcome back to the States dinner."

Mischicot smiled. The rest of their conversation in the car was in French.

"So I've done a lot of research on this Benoit fellow," Mischicot said, "and he looks ripe. My only concern is if he doesn't want to part with his system, then we'll have another Serrano and Malloy on her hands."

"Seffy, you can't buy up all the landmine spotting systems, you know."

"But I can try, can't I? If I don't, those systems will put us out of business. We don't need anyone trying to get rid of landmines when we can sell them to countries still fighting. Have they found that woman yet?"

"No. But it's been three weeks, so maybe she fell down a cliff, was eaten by a bear or wolf, or drowned?"

"No, I think she's alive. I think she might have hurt herself, and someone took her in and is guarding her until she has enough strength to tell her story."

"You really think she's alive?"

"That's just my guess. We need Andrew's bunch to search around that cabin area again. She might be staying in an empty cabin, one of those corporate ones where they still maintain food inventory."

They reached Ramashka's house, and Ramashka and

Mischicot hugged and kissed like they hadn't seen each the previous month. The cook was bringing the meal to the table when the doorbell rang.

"Who could that be?" Mischicot asked.

"I have no idea. I'm not expecting any company," Ramashka said.

Both men looked at Chaplin, but she shook her head. Ramashka went to the door. It was a Girl Scout delivering his cookie order. After paying her and bringing in the cookies, all three looked at each other for a pregnant moment and then started laughing.

"I want the Thin Mints!" Chaplin yelled.

"I want the Tagalongs," Mischicot yelled.

The cook looked at all three.

"Children, that's what you all are. Children!"

After dinner, Mischicot got down to business.

"We meet this Benoit guy tomorrow at nine p.m. Why so late, and why in that godforsaken neighborhood?"

"Two things, Seffy," Ramashka responded. "One, it's in a Black neighborhood, so Benoit feels safe. Second, the hotel doesn't have overnight guests but will accommodate four rooms for us which means unlimited booze, cigars, and cards if we want. The woman who owns the hotel is French, so language will not be a burden in any sense of the word."

"Benoit will have his spotting system with him?"

"He'll have his prototype with him. I guess he doesn't trust too many people."

"Is he coming with anyone?"

"Don't know. However, the hotel owner is his special friend who is very handy with the 'Saturday Night Special' she supposedly hides under her dress."

"Who is this hotel owner?"

Ramashka looked at Chaplin.

"Her name is Camille Bosche. She's coming straight from New Orleans to be with Monsieur Benoit."

"Why is her hotel not open the rest of the year?"

"Madame Bosche inherited the hotel from family and will be putting it out to pasture soon. So, along with Monsieur Benoit, we are in for a special, if not interesting, evening."

***

Billy suggested that Marty view his guest from a distance, and if it is Paula Malloy, Marty should speak with her.

The look on Marty's face said it all to Billy.

"It's her, Billy. Oh my God, it's Paula."

"Okay, Marty, I'll walk her to the post office to continue our little field trip of the grounds. You walk in several minutes later and maybe greet her like you usually do."

"So perhaps I'll help jog her memory?" he asked.

"Yes, what do you think?"

"There could be consequences, Billy. If another person, maybe her dead colleague was involved, the memory might send her into a permanent shock. I don't know."

Billy absorbed what Marty was saying and thought it had merit.

"But you know what, Billy? My girl at the university is a Ph.D. in psychology. Would you mind if she comes over and helps us with this?"

"When could she get here? Is she Indian?"

"She's Indian. I'll call her now."

***

Three-story white-brick "The Anne Hotel" was built in 1840; a beautiful property that was part of history. It served admirably as a hospital during the Civil War and is rumored to have had some involvement in the Underground Railroad. The Anne went from entertaining the well-to-do of Baltimore society for almost 130 years until the murder of Martin Luther King, Jr. in 1968, which led to the Baltimore riots. The neighborhood became unrecognizable after several days and nights of looting and bombings. But The Anne stood her ground.

The great-great-granddaughter of the original owners decided to place The Anne up for sale after several decades of being boarded up.

Because the owner was life-long friends with Al Marino's wife, Ellie, she allowed the FBI to perform the sting operation in The Anne…as long as the FBI did not cause any damage, inside or out, or invite anyone outside the "operation."

Although its six elegant bedrooms were brought into the twenty-first century and all furnished with gas fireplaces, they were still tastefully appointed with antiques from the late nineteenth and early twentieth centuries. The owner thought the FBI sting operation would allow The Anne to participate in one last memorable adventure in her history.

Of course, Marino chuckled.

Two days before the sting, Callahan and Millhouse's three agents toured every nook and cranny with the owner. Callahan felt a little misty-eyed, knowing the historic hotel was for sale. Of course, *she* wasn't going to buy it.

Tim made sure that Callahan and Ahmad practiced their script three straight days before their performance. He felt secure knowing that Howard and Millhouse would be joining him with headphones at an abandoned mansion down the street from The Anne.

A generator would supply the electricity in the hotel starting the morning of the operation. Female undercover agents dressed as maids would make the beds and provide the linens, dishes, glassware, ice, liquor, charcuterie, playing cards, and Cuban cigars. Everyone was ready.

***

Billy was, to say the least, deeply disappointed when Marty told him that his colleague was on a retreat with others in her department and wouldn't return for three more days. Bad timing.

He instantly drew an analogy from when he was ten years old, coming home from school with all A's and was told his parents and older brother died in a car accident. Shortly thereafter he was shipped unwillingly to Piscataway Indian Nation to live with his maternal grandparents, uncles, and aunts.

At twelve years old, Billy was required to go on a vision quest. He was hesitant at first because many boys do not get their vision the first, or sometimes even the second time they venture out. But Billy received his vision on the first try because his mother and father descended from a cloud and spoke to him. They wanted him to get all the education requirements regarding farming and, more importantly, help his people reconnect from intertribal conflict. The elders believed Billy when he returned from the quest.

"What do you want to do, Billy?" Marty asked.

"You go home, Marty, and I'll ask my grandparents for advice. I don't know if I want Paula to see you and her memory connects with whatever negative happened to her, and she descends lower into her spirit, as grandfather says."

"Okay. But should I return tomorrow or when my colleague returns?"

"I'll call you tomorrow and cement our plans. Paula isn't going anywhere soon, but now that I know who she is, we have to keep her safe, and right here on Native property, she is probably the safest."

Marty nodded, and Billy walked him to his car. Afterward, he walked into the longhouse where his grandmother was snapping string beans, and Paula was helping her. His grandfather was walking in with his fishing lines and several fish so Billy scrambled to help him put away his equipment.

"Grandfather, let's take a walk."

"Okay, Billy," he said, looking somewhat puzzled. "I'll meet you outside."

They walked and said nothing for about fifty yards when Billy stopped suddenly.

"Grandfather, I know the woman's name and yes, it was her colleague who washed up on the rocks at the lighthouse."

"What?" he said in an almost unbelievable tone.

"You remember Martin Sheridan, my friend from undergraduate school?"

"Yes, yes, go on."

"Paula, her name is Paula…was assisting Marty for over a year with Ojibwa memorization for his Ph.D. in languages and history."

"That is why she is familiar with Algonquin language."

"Yes, the problem is Paula's amnesia. I think that if she sees Marty…."

"Her spirit will either come back to the surface or descend to depths we cannot reach."

"Yes, Grandfather. I would say contact authorities, but if you recall, the law enforcement agencies we dealt with to report her co-worker's death tried to make us out as the bad guys, like we had something to do with his demise."

"Okay, Billy, we will get the people together tonight and communicate with our ancestors for an answer. You must join us."

"Thank you, Grandfather."

***

It was not easy talking the clan into a meeting for discussion regarding a non-Indian. Although Paula was a Black woman, and most felt she was a lovely person, she was still a non-Indian. The elders thought her being on their land would bring unnecessary law enforcement that was not needed and especially not wanted.

Although his grandfather spoke eloquently about the need to save an innocent, it was Billy who they listened to with open minds. Billy talked about being lost at ten years old and only being able to find his way with the help of the Piscataway Nation.

"Remember, you found her too," he said, looking at the various elders. "You never once considered leaving her in the mud, face down, to die—not once. You thought she deserved better. By now, you must know that she is not just any visitor, she is our divine intervention."

Billy left the group so the elders could pray. He felt his parents were watching and smiling.

***

Howard, Tim, and Millhouse donned headphones as they sat on folding chairs in the big, empty, dank mansion down the street from The Anne Hotel. They took turns going outside to eat because they didn't want to invite any rodents near them...which one of them saw. The only light illuminating their room came from their cellphones and the one flashlight that Tim thought to bring.

Down the street at The Anne Hotel, the plan was working perfectly. Benoit's guests arrived on time. Camille Bosche, the owner, welcomed them in a refined style, offering a charcuterie tray, cigars, and the finest cognac on the market. Callahan and Ahmad were shocked to see the party included Carla Chaplin.

"Why is she here?" Callahan whispered to Ahmad in the kitchen.

All he could do was shake his head in response. He then texted Tim to apprise him of Chaplin's presence. All conversations throughout the night continued in French. Ramashka tried keeping up. The staff fulfilled every request as politely and quickly as they could. After a lengthy Q&A, Mischicot asked Ahmad to produce his prototype, which he did to rave review. It worked seamlessly.

"We are quite interested in your invention, Monsieur Benoit," Mischicot announced. "Is there an opportunity that we can purchase the rights, or at least grant us a gentleman's chance to buy in?"

"I am in awe of your compliment, Monsieur Mischicot. But so that you know, I am mainly here because

I was curious as to how you knew I was creating such a product."

Benoit looked over at Chaplin.

"Monsieur Benoit," she began. "As you have surely checked us out, you must know that we are proven authorities in the IT field and try our best to stay ahead of the future. Some of your competitors currently racing to the patent office also know of your invention. It is a small, exclusive club but, as you can see, not so private. We want to offer you one million dollars in cash for your spotting system. Would this work for you?"

Benoit seemed to be thinking about it for a moment. He then called in his best friend Camille and asked her what she thought of the offer.

"My friends," she said almost sincerely, "Monsieur Benoit has been working on his discovery for almost three years. He is seeking *recognition* of his invention rather than monetary satisfaction, so unless you can grant him the Nobel Prize, I'm afraid one million dollars would not suffice."

"What amount would suffice?" Ramashka asked.

All looked at him as he sipped his cognac.

"No amount at this time, Monsieur…?"

"Ramashka."

He spoke in English; Chaplin translated it in French.

"You see, we believe everyone has a price. Perhaps we have not communicated yours correctly. Could I be right?"

Camille looked over at Benoit.

"We will discuss what a price would look like and inform you of our decision tomorrow," she said. "It is now midnight. Monsieur Benoit and I will be staying overnight.

You are welcome to join us as my staff has prepared rooms for your convenience."

"Madame, we need a minute," Mischicot informed her. "Would you allow us a few moments in private?"

She and Benoit nodded and left the room. Once the "staff" left the room and, by all appearances, trekked upstairs, Mischicot, Ramashka, and Chaplin searched the drawing room and two bathrooms for any mics. They found none. Callahan watched through a hole in the dumbwaiter and could only read Chaplin's lips as Mischicot and Ramashka had their backs to her. However, Howard, Tim, and Millhouse heard mostly Ramashka's and Mischicot's voices because the microphone attached to the bottom of the charcuterie tray, which the guests failed to check, was situated between them. They called "Bosche" and "Benoit" back into the room.

"We will not be staying overnight, Madame," Mischicot said, "but want to thank you for your superb service, especially knowing you have arranged this night for our benefit."

"Monsieur Mischicot, I arranged this night for Monsieur Benoit's benefit."

Mischicot decided to ignore the slight. "I am sorry you are selling this fine hotel. What a shame."

"The way of the world," Camille said, appearing in agony.

"We know how to get in touch with you," Benoit said.

"We will wait for your offer tomorrow, then?" Mischicot asked.

"We will provide you an answer tomorrow," Benoit stated.

The guests departed, getting into the three Mercedes vehicles parked in the circular driveway. Howard, Tim, and Millhouse folded their chairs and dashed out of the mansion as quickly as possible because they could not take one more moment in residence. When the vehicles had become a blur, the agents ran out to Millhouse's sedan, placed the chairs in the trunk, and headed to The Anne Hotel for a late-night conference.

"Wow, that was some get-together," Tim said, sifting through the remains of the charcuterie tray. "You guys were great!"

"I was just thinking," Howard said, "Millhouse, why don't you allow your people to stay here overnight? I think something is going to happen."

"Like what?" Callahan asked.

"Tim, I'd like Ahmad to stay, too."

"What do you think is going to happen, Howard?" Tim asked.

Millhouse smiled.

"I think, Monsieur Benoit, there will be an attempt to kidnap you."

Everyone then sat down and listened to Howard's plan.

***

The elders decided that Paula Malloy's spirit was worth saving. They suggested a plan that involved several steps. First, permit Martin Sheridan's colleague to come to the nation and talk with Paula. If her memory returned, get her story and then contact the police. However, if her memory did not want to return, they would contact her family.

Before the elders took over the prayer, many of the attendees, young people, watched and listened to Billy with almost rapt attention. One of those young people was Liz, the clerk at the post office.

"Billy," she whispered excitedly, "I want to show you something and tell me if I am right."

He looked at her quizzically but followed her to the post office. Once inside, she pointed to Paula's picture on the bulletin board.

"That's her!" Billy said. "Where did you get this picture, Liz?"

"Two FBI people came several days ago and asked me to post this picture because the woman was missing."

"Was one a Black man and the other a white woman with red hair?"

"Yes...Yes."

"Liz, you are wonderful. Thank you. Did they leave a number where I can contact them?"

"Yes, you can ask Lieutenant Swann about it, too, because he met with them."

"Nah, Swann hates the FBI. Trust me on this. He certainly didn't try to help them if he met with them. That's not his style."

"Well, in that case," she said, pointing to the picture. "The FBI guy left his name and number on the back."

Billy carefully removed the picture from the bulletin board, viewed the name and number on the back. He hugged and thanked Liz profusely before running out the door. She beamed from ear to ear as Billy, smiling, took the picture with him.

Realizing it was late evening, Billy should have waited until the following day to place the call, but he was restless. The answering service told him Agent Watson was not in the office. But after listening to the caller's reason for contacting Howard, the service told him she was sure Agent Watson would get back to him promptly.

***

The next morning Billy decided since he hadn't heard from Agent Watson that he would continue his tour of Piscataway territory with Paula as she was feeling better and her sprained ankle was now a non-issue. He mentioned to her that Native Americans have lived along the Patuxent River since 1100 BC. He decided to try an experiment so he walked her to Cat Hole Trail to see if anything jogged her memory. Nothing. But she did later point out the most beautiful flora and the bike trails, mentioning she loved riding her off-road bike. Billy was most intrigued by this slip of the tongue. He made sure he listened carefully. During this trek, they walked near the cliff where she might have fallen, and she became quiet for a moment.

"What is it?" he asked.

"I don't know," she answered. "Something about those beautiful moss-covered boulders down there..."

A little later they came to a bridge over a section of the river that was muddier than the rest. Paula stopped and stared at the water.

"Why do I know this bridge?" she asked.

"Maybe you've been here before? Maybe as a kid?"

"I don't think so," she said, still staring.

She seemed greatly enchanted by the tall brown grasses, moss-covered rocks and boulders, the bluest sky she'd ever seen, and when standing atop Cat Hole Pass, the highest cliff, the sight granted her a panoramic view of trees that dotted the landscape in all directions.

"I love this area," she said, smiling.

Billy had never seen her smile; it was breathtaking.

She was breathtaking. Suddenly, a dog, out of nowhere and dragging a leash ran past them, and she grabbed Billy.

"I feel a little silly right now since I have a dog, so it's not like I'm afraid of them."

She stopped walking.

"Why did I say that?"

"Say what?" he asked.

"Nothing. It's nothing."

They walked back to the village, and even the red dirt on the roads seemed to thrill her.

***

Ahmad woke up in his plush, queen-size bed in The Anne Hotel around four a.m. to what he thought was the sound of glass breaking. He pretended to be asleep. The next thing he knew, a giant hand went over his mouth, and a gun was placed on his head.

"Get slowly out of bed, Mr. Benoit, and don't say nothin' and don't try nothin'," the husky robot-like voice said in English.

Ahmad slowly got out of the bed with the stranger's hand still on his mouth, and the gun still pointed at his head. He could not determine the stranger's appearance as he wore gloves, a black facemask and a black hood, but the man had massive arms, so Ahmad deduced that he was probably a bodybuilder. Ahmad also considered the voice to be a recording. The man removed his hand from Ahmad's mouth but kept the gun pointed at him.

"Put your pants and shoes on now!" he commanded.

Ahmad scrambled to put his clothes on.

"What is happening? Why are you doing this?" he asked in French.

The man then clocked Ahmad with his gun on the side of his head. "Didn't I say don't say nothin'?"

Ahmad felt the blood trickle down the side of his face as duct tape was placed across his mouth. His hands were tied behind him. With a pillowcase over his head, Ahmad was led from the bedroom and down the backstairs of the hotel. He was shoved into the back of a waiting van in the hotel's alley. The man then jumped into the vehicle and joined the driver. The van took off. Callahan crept to her window and made her call.

About three miles later the van turned down a desolate street and pulled into a driveway of a boarded up two-story house. The kidnappers got out of the van and one of them pulled Ahmad out. They headed into the house. The driver made a phone call.

"Yeah, this is me. We got him. What do you want us to do? Take him to the cabin?...at this hour? Okay, okay, okay."

The kidnappers and Ahmad returned to the van, but a sedan driven by Howard blocked its exit in the driveway. The van's driver decided to drive through the backyard to the alley but another sedan was there to greet them. Millhouse was in this sedan. He and his men got out of the car and held out their FBI credentials and their guns at the men in the van.

Millhouse yelled, "FBI. Get out of the vehicle. Throw your weapons on the ground and keep your hands up!"

Millhouse's men then confiscated their guns, cuffed them, then thoroughly searched them, then "helped" them into the sedan. Millhouse's men then drove off with the perpetrators in the backseat.

Howard, Tim, and Millhouse hurried to the van and helped Ahmad. They took off the pillowcase, now stained with blood, and saw that Ahmad was bleeding on the side of his head. It was determined that he would live.

"I didn't think you guys were going to get here in time," he said. "Although I was hoping."

"Millhouse's people had your back, Ahmad," Tim said. "We didn't anticipate your being slapped upside your head, but nothing more was going to happen to you on my watch."

"Thanks, Tim."

"Don't thank me, this was Howard's plan, remember?"

All four men got in Howard's car, and he drove off.

***

Marino and Kramer were in Fleischman's office detailing the strategy leading to the operation's success. Of course, they had to explain the reason for the modified game plan too.

"The next step is to slap Mischicot, Ramashka, and Chaplin with cuffs. But how do we do this carefully?" Fleischman asked.

"If only we could hit them with something harder than trying to buy off a scientist," Marino said with a sigh. "If just one of their wrestlers talk, we could add kidnapping charges."

"I don't see that happening, Al," Kramer added.

Marino's executive assistant, Wendy, was on Fleischman's speakerphone.

"Director, a young man is here to see Agent Watson, who is not in the office today."

"Did he have an appointment with Watson?" Fleischman asked.

"No, but based on his reason for being here, I suggest the chief talk to him."

Marino looked at Kramer in amused puzzlement. He nodded to Fleischman to let him in.

"Thank you, Wendy, have someone escort him up to my office."

Billy entered Fleischman's office and was directed to a seat on the sofa.

"Yessir, how can we help you, Mr…?" Marino asked.

"Savoy. Billy Savoy."

He then produced a picture of Paula Malloy.

"I am of the Piscataway Indian Nation near the lower Patuxent, and I have been waiting for your Agent Watson to call me back but since he hasn't, I decided I'd come to him. Is this the scientist you are looking for? If so, she has been with us for almost three weeks and—"

"Well, why didn't you contact us sooner so we could stop looking?" Fleischman said in a somewhat irritated tone.

Marino wanted to slug him.

"Mr. Savoy," Marino interrupted, "how long have you known she was who we were looking for?"

"Not long, sir. Dr. Malloy was found at the bottom of Cat Hole Trail on Piscataway grounds, face down in the mud. We believe she fell from a cliff and hit her head on a boulder. She was cuffed from behind, and duct tape was on her mouth. She has amnesia, so it was hard to know where she came from and, more importantly, who she was."

"Why didn't you call the authorities anyway?" Fleischman asked.

Billy quickly understood why Lieutenant Swann despised the FBI. He glared at Fleischman.

"Because we didn't know who her enemy was at the time."

"And you know who her enemy is now?"

"You probably don't know this, but my grandfather and I were the two fishermen who pulled her colleague, Dr. Serrano, from the Chesapeake three weeks ago. Only recently did we notice similarities in him and Dr. Malloy, but we weren't sure, so we took care of her. She was badly bruised. We thought she would emerge from her amnesia, but she hasn't. I learned your Agent Watson visited our nation several days ago and left this picture of Dr. Malloy in our post office. I did not know until yesterday that our guest is, in fact, Dr. Malloy."

"How do you know so much about Dr. Serrano, Mr. Savoy?" Marino asked.

"I read everything I could going through the various newspapers for the article about his death."

Marino looked at Kramer.

"Our elders believe whoever killed Dr. Serrano is still looking for Dr. Malloy or her body," Billy said with controlled elocution. "My only question is should we keep her in our settlement until you find the people who did this to her and Dr. Serrano, or do we notify her family?"

"Mr. Savoy, thank you so much for this information," Marino began. "Yes, keep Dr. Malloy in your village until we get in touch with Agent Watson. He will be delighted to know this turn of events. We will not contact her family…yet, but they must know that their family member is alive. Please leave contact information so that Agent Watson can get in touch with you."

Fleischman felt he had to speak. "On behalf of the FBI, I want to thank you for bringing us this information and, more importantly, protecting Dr. Malloy. I'm sure her family will be forever grateful. Citizens like you make our job so much easier."

Billy almost smiled at what he deemed was a canned compliment. Before leaving, he parted with his digits for Agent Watson.

***

In addition to their teams, Howard and Millhouse also took the day off. Good news greeted Howard when he strolled into Marino's office the next morning. He had been waiting to hear for twenty-two days that Dr. Paula Malloy was alive.

"You were right about the Piscataway and Serrano connection, Howard," Marino said, pouring himself a cup of coffee. "But what made you make the connection?"

"I can't explain it, Al. I thought the two Indians who called authorities to report Dr. Serrano's death were just good people."

"What do you mean?"

"Since Dr. Serrano's body washed ashore near Piscataway territory, I thought perhaps Dr. Malloy was also on or near Piscataway land. Maybe she and Serrano were escaping together from that cabin until something happened to separate them. And where better to hide than on Indian land? It was just a guess. I got lucky."

"Yeah, that was some luck. What will you do now?"

"Give this Billy Savoy a call, take Dr. Tanaka with me—"

"Our clinical Psych?"

"Yep, the same one, and see what Dr. Paula Malloy has to say."

"Good luck. Call me when you're heading back to DC."

****

To say Mischicot was livid when he heard two of Sweeten's men had been arrested was putting it mildly.

"How the hell did the Feds know about the plans? Who the hell talked?" he yelled.

Chaplin and Ramashka looked at each other, knowing that neither had breached that divide.

"I believe the Feds were probably following Sweeten, Seffy. He's still on their radar."

"You don't know that for sure, Carla," Ramashka added. "You're just guessing because you can't stand him."

"I can't stand him, Bobo, because he's a fuckup."

"Have we heard from Andrew?" Mischicot asked.

"Not yet, but you know we will, Seffy," Ramashka replied. "And besides, Andrew wasn't near the hotel when the plan began or ended. Why would he set up his own men unless one was a traitor?"

"It still doesn't make sense how the Feds knew the house," Chaplin said. "Anyway, those wrestlers won't talk. We've promised them a hefty price if they don't talk."

"Carla, dear," Mischicot said almost too sincerely, "kidnapping is a federal crime. They'll talk, and they'll talk to get reduced to no sentences, which will enable them to continue their wrestling careers."

"Well, the only person in this equation that will hang us besides Dr. Malloy is now Andrew Sweeten."

With this statement, Chaplin brought an inconvenient truth to the surface.

***

Andrew Sweeten heard about the botched kidnapping and knew he would be the fall guy.

"Not this time," he said to the mirror. "Not this time."

He called Mischicot.

"I have no idea how the Feds knew our plan. Somebody talked and it wasn't me."

"We *will* get to the bottom of this, Andrew."

"I hope so and soon because I know where that woman scientist is," he said.

"Where, Andrew?" Mischicot asked excitedly. "And how do you know this?"

"She's on Indian land outside of Baltimore. My canary told me she has amnesia or something like that after taking a tumble down a cliff. You want us to go get her?"

"So this is why we couldn't find her. Will the Indians let us get close to her? Or do we take her at night?"

"I have a plan, and my canary will help us."

"For how much, Andrew?"

"Five grand, okay?"

***

Camille Bosche sent a direct message to the covert link suggesting $2 million in cash for Monsieur Benoit's invention. She waited almost a day for the return message.

"The meeting will be Monday at seven p.m. at Global Tectronics in Crofton," Callahan wrote back.

"We have three days to make this work," Howard told Marino over the phone. "Callahan needs to attend the meeting and say Mr. Benoit told the FBI that he has decided his life is worth more than the invention, so he's selling it because someone tried to kidnap him for it."

***

Howard and Dr. Margaret Tanaka drove into Piscataway territory with many eyes focused on their car. Billy and Marty were already waiting for both. Billy hurried over to meet Howard as soon as he got out of the vehicle. Marty helped Dr. Tanaka out of the car.

"Thank you for coming, Agent Watson…Dr. Tanaka," he said enthusiastically.

"No, Mr. Savoy, thank you for what you're doing and for what you've done for Dr. Malloy."

Billy and Marty escorted them to the library where they would not be interrupted. Billy told them how the elders found Dr. Malloy several days before he and his grandfather found Dr. Serrano's body washed up on the lighthouse.

"We didn't correlate the two incidents for a while until I searched for the article about Dr. Serrano's body being identified. Sure, we noticed Dr. Serrano's hands were cuffed behind his back and that duct tape had almost completely come off his mouth from the water, but as I said, we did not need nor want any trouble with law enforcement. NCIS almost made my grandfather and me out to be the bad guys."

"What happened next?" Howard asked.

"When Dr. Malloy didn't know who she was or where she was from, we had to walk delicately around her as she was between two worlds, and my grandfather did not want her to return to this world remembering a negative incident that sent her there in the first place. As it is, many times, she has nightmares about someone being hurt. We figured it must have been Dr. Serrano."

"Has she given you any indication that she remembers anything prior to your finding her?" Dr. Tanaka asked.

"She recalls certain things, but not many," Billy answered.

"That's good to know," Dr. Tanaka remarked. "First, I would like to meet your grandparents. Afterward, we should have Mr. Sheridan say hello to Dr. Malloy, and then let's see what happens from there."

***

Dr. Tanaka was quite impressed with Billy's grandparents, especially his grandmother. They had a lot to say to each other as they were alone for almost thirty minutes. When both emerged from their informal conversation, Dr. Tanaka asked to see Paula.

When she first viewed the young woman, she felt that the Indians had taken good care of her. She also felt that the cocoon they protected her in might unravel once she learned why she was there on Indian land. But Dr. Tanaka had to see from what stock the woman was built. She asked Marty to walk into the longhouse with Billy, call her name, and start talking.

"But what do I say?" Marty asked her.

"What would you normally say when acknowledging her presence, Mr. Sheridan?" she asked. "The point is that you haven't seen her for a while and want to know what she's doing now."

Marty, along with Billy, walked into the longhouse and saw Paula helping Billy's grandmother set the table. He called over and walked toward her. "Paula, is that you?"

She looked confused. "Are you talking to me?" she answered.

"Yes, it's Martin…Marty Sheridan. You don't remember me?"

She looked at Billy, then back to him.

"No, I'm sorry, I don't. Forgive me, but I don't remember you."

Dr. Tanaka gave Marty the "let it go" sign.

"It's okay. You probably meet many people. No

problem."

He then walked out of the longhouse with Billy, and Paula continued setting the table.

Dr. Tanaka met Howard, Billy, the grandfather, and Marty outside near Howard's car.

"She hasn't quite grasped the situation yet. Billy, if you say she pointed out several familiar things on your walk the other day, perhaps certain pertinent revelations are happening."

Dr. Tanaka was about to continue talking when Paula yelled from the front porch, "Grandfather, Grandmother says it is time for lunch and to bring your guests. Billy, bring Marty, too, if he has time." She went back into the house.

They were all stunned except Dr. Tanaka.

***

"Are you sure, Seffy?" she asked.

"Yes, Carla, we're sure. Andrew has an Indian friend heading their police department who told him about the scientist. She has some form of amnesia from falling down a cliff, which is why she hasn't talked to the authorities. I guess some of the Indians have been taking care of her."

"What's our plan, Seffy? Because, if her amnesia retreats, she can certainly identify Sweeten, who will not take the fall, no matter how much money we offer."

"That's probably true. The guy wants five grand. Should we do this, Carla? Bobo is on board, but what about you?"

"I don't know, Seffy. I'm afraid of prison."

"Carla, I thought we were mates. I thought I could count on you through thick and thin. Please don't leave me hanging, as you Americans like to say."

"Okay, Seffy, but I need to see a real plan."

"Come to Bobo's tonight, and we'll get specific. I love you, Carla."

That's all she needed to hear.

***

Billy Savoy's parents left the Piscataway Indian Nation while they were in graduate school at Johns Hopkins University in Baltimore. The intertribal fighting became too much for both. After their move they landed jobs in the Information Technology field. Billy's older brother Charlie was born two days after both parents received their master's degrees. Billy was born two years later. Billy's mother shared a somewhat healthy relationship with her parents, but his father's parents refused to speak to him once he left the Nation.

When Billy's parents and brother were killed in a car accident when he was ten, he went to live with his mother's parents on the Piscataway settlement land near the lower Patuxent. At age eighteen, he received the trust fund left by his parents, which he used for undergraduate and graduate schools. At twenty-five, he received the balance of the trust, which he used to buy his trailer and a fishing boat for his grandfather. He taught at the local community college for two years before being accepted into Purdue University's doctoral program in Indiana.

Billy balanced both his Piscataway life and the world of academia without a hitch. His vision never wavered. He only needed to get the requirements from education to learn everything he could about running a farming concern efficiently and especially profitably. He was on his way.

Paula Malloy was, however, the crack in his armor. He had only known her for twenty-three days, but he really liked her. What if she didn't get well? What if they had to contact her family and she had to leave the settlement...and him?

He thought about these issues and wondered if he was throwing her to the wolves. Purdue would start in a month; he would be getting robed in five months. Someone, or someones, still wanted her dead. How could he leave here without knowing she would be in good hands?

***

Andrew Sweeten, his two thugs, and the tribal deputy officer met at the cabin.

"We need to get rid of Billy Savoy, her self-appointed protector," the deputy told them. "That's the only way you can grab her."

The deputy told them that Billy and his team were always perusing the grounds early in the morning, deciding what to grow and which specific fields, securing meetings in Baltimore for financing options, and staying up to date on the latest farm animals and equipment.

"It has to be in two days," he said. "That's when Billy goes into Baltimore."

The deputy wanted half of the agreed-upon money upfront, but Sweeten told him he'd give him *all* the money when they completed the job. The deputy reluctantly agreed.

***

After everyone had finished the fine but simple meal set out by Billy's grandmother, it was time for Howard, Dr. Tanaka, and Marty to head back to DC and Baltimore. Dr. Tanaka was not surprised that Paula did not say anything to summon up intimacy or attachment. She then took the grandmother aside and asked in an almost whisper.

"Did you purposely tell Dr. Malloy to invite all of us to lunch?"

"Yes," the grandmother said. "I thought Martin would bring something inside her to the surface. I was right to do this, yes?"

"Yes, you were, and thank you. I believe certain things are coming back slowly."

Once Howard and Dr. Tanaka hit the road, Howard had a slew of questions.

"Margaret, do you think she's faking the amnesia?"

"At first, I wasn't quite sure, but later I found her to be legit because I could tell she was processing all her answers."

"What do you think? Should we call her family? Is it time for them to retrieve her?"

"That's going to be tricky. First, Billy's family is her protection, and she believes she needs protecting, she just doesn't know why. Second, her life is in grave danger, and sooner rather than later, the tongues here will wag outside this fort, and those looking for her will find her. Also, probably most importantly, her family needs to know she is alive."

Howard blew out steam. "Marino isn't gonna like this."

***

Chaplin met Mischicot at Ramashka's house. Sweeten arrived fifteen minutes later, and Chaplin looked at him with disgust. He glared at her menacingly.

"Get your ass off your shoulders."

Mischicot had had enough. "If you talk to her like that again, Andrew, I will tear out your throat. Do you understand?"

Sweeten shrugged and took a seat on the couch.

"Now, what's the plan?" he asked.

After Sweeten got over the verbal whipping he laid out the plan.

"With the help of my Indian friend at that reservation, we'll grab the woman and drive her back to the cabin. After we tie her up, we throw her into the Chesapeake. It's that simple."

"And you're sure this Indian friend of yours believes we can do this without anyone seeing you or even stopping you?"

"Yes. This time, I'll handle the details."

"I think we should be at the cabin to make sure," Ramashka piped in.

"I'm inclined to agree with Bobo, Andrew," Mischicot declared.

Sweeten shrugged. "Whatever."

Chaplin had a thought. "If the woman actually has amnesia, then she won't remember the incident or even Andrew's thugs. So why the rush?"

"No rush, really," Ramashka added. "However, if and when her memory is restored, she'll remember everything and everyone. Why not just beat the buzzer? Besides, we haven't heard anything or read anything about her disappearance or death, have we?"

Sweeten thought about this question. "Well, I did see something about a week ago about a memorial for her until her body is recovered."

Ramashka was furious. "Why didn't you mention this to any of us?"

"Because I didn't know it was this same chick. My Indian friend told me it was the same woman only yesterday and that the article was bogus. The article was like only two sentences and only mentioned that this woman had drowned. I told you, Seffy."

Chaplin and Ramashka looked at Mischicot.

"He told me *last night.* That's why we're here today," Mischicot replied. "Andrew, what day and time is your plan supposed to happen?"

"Tuesday morning. It seems her protector goes into Baltimore on Tuesday mornings for some financial meetings, and I'm told that's the best time, with him off that reservation."

Mischicot pondered the explanation. "That only gives us two days to make sure nothing stupid happens."

Sweeten continued. "Her bodyguard, so to speak, leaves the plantation at eight thirty a.m., so I suggest we grab her at nine."

All three agreed with Sweeten's suggestion.

"Okay, Andrew, we have other things to work on, so we'll see you at that cabin between nine thirty and ten?"

Sweeten nodded. He then bid everyone au revoir and departed their company. Chaplin looked at Ramashka and

Mischicot.

"I have a bad feeling about this, you guys," she said. "Maybe we shouldn't go to that cabin."

Both men pondered her statement with reluctance.

"What time do we meet Benoit, Carla?" Ramashka asked.

"Tomorrow at seven p.m., in the basement of Global. We have the money…right?"

Mischicot bobbed his head and looked at Ramashka.

"I was thinking," Mischicot said. "Let's only offer Benoit $750 thousand because the attempted kidnapping scared him and I'm of the opinion he'll take anything at this time. What do you think?"

Ramashka nodded. "I was thinking the same, Seffy."

***

"Agent Watson, I realize I am calling you on a Sunday, but is there any chance you and Dr. Tanaka can come to the Nation?"

That was the message left on Howard's service board. It was Sunday, and he didn't want to return the call but knew something was up. Eventually, he returned the call on his work cellphone—the one the recipient would see as "Unknown."

"Mr. Savoy, this is Howard Watson. Is there something wrong? Did something happen?"

"Thank you, Agent Watson, for returning my call. Yes, I think Paula…Dr. Malloy has found her voice, at least a portion of it."

"If so," Howard replied, "we'll be there in the morning."

Then it hit Howard like a brick. "Oh, Mr. Savoy, I am sorry. We can't be there tomorrow, but we can be there on Tuesday morning…will this work?"

"Yes, yes. I know this is asking a lot, but can you come early, because I have a final finance meeting in Baltimore at nine thirty? If you can be here at eight a.m., that would really work. Is this at all possible?"

"I will check with Dr. Tanaka and get back to you if we cannot meet you. At this moment, we'll be there."

"Thank you, Agent Watson."

When Howard ended the call, he got up from the desk in his study and walked over to the window, and stared out at his thirteen-year-old twin boys shooting hoops in the driveway. He also noticed his wife Carol chatting over the fence with their next-door neighbors. Howard wondered what he and his wife would do if one of their children went missing. He could not shake the thought. Dr. Malloy's family had to know that she was alive.

***

Everyone met in Kramer's conference room in Baltimore.

"Just so we're all clear," Kramer began, "this is Terrence's and Watson's meeting. Al and I are only here for the donut holes."

Of course, the chuckling was contagious.

"Millhouse and Howard are here to outline the evening's plan to hopefully collect extortion money from Mischicot, Ramashka, and Chaplin."

Millhouse pointed to Ahmad, who was smiling. "We are being optimistic that the three pawns will try to shakedown our Mr. Benoit here. And that's when we haul them in on charges stemming from mail fraud, extortion, and kidnapping. They, of course, will think one of Sweeten's wrestlers talked. Our two moves down the chessboard will involve charging Ms. Chaplin with securities fraud for lying to her shareholders on what they were actually investing in, which is the micro processing boards...for landmines. The court will view Ms. Chaplin's crime of lying in terms of how it may have impacted her company and shareholders. Questions."

Hands went up in the air.

"Yamamoto."

"Thanks, Millhouse. Kudos to our whistleblower at Global Tectronics, but what do we hope to gain with the shakedown?"

"Good question. We will probably close the company to allow the shareholders to go after Chaplin. If she takes the bullet for the parent company, Mischicot's *family's* company in France, I'd say she's built better than I thought.

However, I don't see her going down with the ship."

Another hand in the air.

"Hamilton."

"If the pawns offer Ahmad, I mean Mr. Benoit, less than what he's asking, should Benoit refuse the offer?"

"Absolutely. Our perps probably believe that Benoit is scared because of the recent attempted kidnapping. They'll be of the opinion that Benoit would now rather have the money and return to Haiti with a hefty bank account."

Another hand in the air.

"Waverly."

"Am I going to be strapped this time?"

The room erupted in laughter.

"Yes, you are, Agent Waverly. By the way, Callahan will not participate in this part of the mission because those bimbos believe Camille is smarter than Benoit, who they believe they can easily take for a ride if she's not around. So she won't be around."

This explanation didn't sit comfortably with Tim.

"Millhouse, you know Callahan would want to be part of the finish line in this operation. She thinks on her feet, plays poker, can read lips, and is a bomb tech. What more can you ask? She was our saving grace at The Anne."

Everyone in the room nodded.

"What do you think, Howard?"

"I'd say let's use her lip-reading abilities. Al, do we have enough in the budget for Callahan to return?"

Marino and Kramer stopped chomping on donut holes.

Marino was straightforward with his answer. "Yeah, I'll call her supervisor."

Smiles all around the room.

"If it's okay with you, Howard," Millhouse stated, "could our teams meet at eighteen thirty at that diner in Crofton where we met Callahan?"

"It works for me."

They all filed out of the room. Howard stopped Brett and Kevin before they got to the elevators.

"Brett, I need you and Kevin to accompany Dr. Tanaka and me tomorrow early to Piscataway territory."

"Sure, Howard," Brett said. "How early?"

"Let's leave here at oh seven thirty."

Kevin's eyes went wide.

"Any special reason for that hour?"

"No, Kevin, just eager to please the request of a wonderful citizen who I can't turn down."

PART THREE

A large plume of smoke was visible a half-mile before Howard and Millhouse, and their teams, reached the Global Tectronics building. Four fire trucks were there, blocking all access to the building. Officials told Millhouse that the fire was mostly confined to the roof but did enter at least one top-floor office, triggering the sprinklers. The official asked not to go on record but believed someone did not accurately extinguish the barbecue grills on the building's roof deck.

The fire canceled the rendezvous. Everyone went home to wait for another message for another day.

After Howard and Millhouse arrived at the cafe near headquarters, Howard looked searchingly at Millhouse.

"What are the odds?" he asked.

"I don't know, Howard. We could chalk it up to coincidence, but you and I are not from that camp, are we? But why would they go to such expense to cancel this meeting?"

Howard thought about the question. "As Al often says, it could be simple—it could have just been a fire."

***

The three met at Ramashka's house. They could still see the black smoke from a mile away. Needless to say, Mischicot was livid. He had mentioned to Chaplin several times about the employees grilling on the roof and not following safety guidelines. *Several times*. Now he had to be blunt.

"You just gave my grandfather more ammunition for why women should not be in charge."

"Seffy…" She couldn't go on…so she didn't.

"What do we do now?" Ramashka asked.

"We regroup. Since the fire was on the top floor, the fire department said we should give the employees the rest of the week off to provide the disaster cleanup specialists time to remedy this mess and hopefully restore our property to its original condition."

"Do we reschedule with Benoit?"

"Yes, Bobo, take care of this. Just remember, we can't meet him tomorrow."

***

Howard was already in bed when Callahan called. As soon as he answered, she immediately began begging.

"Howard, I'm so sorry to be calling this late, but before you say no, I was thinking, since the fire at Global botched our operation, can I accompany you and Dr. Tanaka tomorrow to Piscataway?"

He groaned loud enough for Carol to turn over in the bed and give him that "please take this into your study" look.

He walked into his study while on his phone. "Callahan, we already have four in my car…"

"I can follow you if you let me. I, too, want to see this part of the operation shut down. And if luck is on our side, maybe Dr. Malloy will say who did this to her and Dr. Serrano."

"All right, we leave from headquarters at oh seven thirty. I won't wait, Callahan."

***

Mischicot, Ramashka, and Chaplin rode together to the cabin.

"Let's get something to eat. I'm starving," Chaplin announced.

"There are several places along the way," Ramashka said. "We can take our food to the cabin while we wait for Sweeten and his quarry."

*****

Howard and company pulled into the village at eight fifteen, drove to the library as instructed, and parked. Inside the library were Billy, the grandparents, and Marty. Paula did not want to meet; no matter how much they tried to persuade her, she would not leave the longhouse.

Howard had to ask. "Why was it so imperative we had to come here, Mr. Savoy?"

"She...Paula said she didn't want those men to find her. I asked her, what men? She said, 'those men who want me dead.'"

"What sparked this conversation?" Dr. Tanaka asked.

"We were walking by a grove of corn, and Paula stopped suddenly. I asked what was wrong, and she said, they're going to find me, aren't they? I said who, who's going to find you? She didn't say anything else."

Dr. Tanaka looked at Howard and said, "She's coming back to us. We have to be ready with the onslaught of emotions."

"Should we all be in her presence?" Howard asked. "What do you think, Doc?"

Dr. Tanaka looked at all the worried faces. "Howard, this is your call."

***

Andrew Sweeten and two of his thugs rode in his black SUV. They were on their way to meet with the Tribal deputy officer at Cattail Bridge, about 200 yards from the Municipal Square. The deputy told them to park near the bridge, follow any trees with a blue ribbon attached to a branch on foot, and meet up with him at nine. As soon as Malloy's bodyguard left the settlement, they would go in and grab her.

***

Lieutenant Swann was more than unhappy. He was on his way to the longhouse because he had just learned from the postal clerk that Paula Malloy was the missing person staying with Billy Savoy's grandparents. He decided to walk instead of drive, possibly surprising them and threatening the grandparents with expulsion from the Nation for harboring a "so-called" kidnapped hostage. However, as he passed the library, he noticed several sedans parked behind it. He chuckled because everybody knew a "cop car."

Before he moved in the direction of the library, Swann also noticed his deputy walking down Red Dirt Lane and was quite puzzled that he was up so early because his shift didn't start until late afternoon. Swann was curious to know where the deputy was going at this early hour, so he followed. He stood behind some trees and watched his deputy talk to three Black men. Who were they? And why were they strapped?

Then he saw the black SUV and recalled Agent Watson's story. It hit him like a ton of bricks. He then reached for his phone and took pictures. He quietly dashed out of the woods and headed to the library.

He entered the library as everyone was ready to walk over to the longhouse.

"Agents," he said. "Thought I'd find you here. Something's getting ready to go down. Where is your Dr. Malloy right now?" he asked Billy.

"She's…she's…"

"She's in the longhouse," Howard answered. "Why,

what's going down?"

"Agent Watson, you mentioned a black SUV. I believe I saw my deputy talking with some hoodlum-type fellas, some fellas over in the woods, and I think my deputy has thrown your Dr. Malloy under the bus. I took some pictures."

He showed them to Howard…who then told his people to lock and load.

All the agents checked their weapons, including Callahan. Howard barked out orders.

"Dr. Tanaka, Mr. Sheridan, stay in this library. Do not venture out until one of us returns for you both. Do you understand me?"

"Yes," they said in unison.

Billy looked at his grandparents, who seemed scared. "What do you want me and my grandparents to do, Agent Watson?"

Howard took a moment. "Where were you going this morning, which required us to come early?"

"I go into Baltimore every Tuesday for a financing seminar. This would have been my final class. But I'm sure—"

"No, Billy, I want you to leave the territory just like you planned. You don't have to go to Baltimore, you just have to leave here. Whoever is after Dr. Malloy knows you'll be going to Baltimore."

"Are you sure, Agent Watson? I mean, who's going to protect Paula if I'm not here?"

"Exactly, Billy," Lieutenant Swann butted in. "They knew you were leaving, and I'm sure my deputy filled them in on your schedule."

He went over to the wall and slammed it with his fist. "Money, the root of all evil."

Howard agreed. He looked over at Billy. "Billy, you have a cell phone, right? We'll text you when it's time to come home. Do not under any circumstances try to contact me. Let us take care of this. Don't be stupid and try to be a hero, because you will be a dead one. Now go get your truck and leave."

Billy went into the longhouse, picked up his briefcase, saw Paula, waved good bye, hopped into his truck, and left the settlement.

Howard continued. "Grandparents, I want you to return to the longhouse. I do not want you in the house with Dr. Malloy. Do whatever you usually do, hang out the clothes, clean fishing tackle, clean fish, prepare meals…whatever you usually do but stay outside. Do not in any way try to be heroes. We will ensure no harm comes to you or Dr. Malloy as long as you follow my instructions. Do you both understand me?"

Both nodded and began their trek to the longhouse.

Howard mapped out a plan for Brett, Kevin, Callahan, and Lieutenant Swann. Now all they had to do was wait.

***

"Why do we have to kill her, Seffy, especially if she has amnesia? She doesn't know who she is, where she's from, or if she has any family."

"Carla, getting rid of her will be the only way to protect you, me, and Bobo. She knows what Andrew and his two men look like, and if she identifies Andrew, or one, or both of his men, they'll surely give us up. Dead people can't talk, otherwise, Serrano's death would have led them to us. Stop being emotional about this. You didn't care this much about Dr. Serrano, and we didn't even kill him. He had a heart attack and departed this life before we threw him into the Chesapeake."

"I cared. I'm just sorry that Sweeten and his men didn't keep their masks on. I don't know. I still feel a chill about this woman."

"Let's map out a new date for Benoit and move on. Bobo, how's that coming?"

"It's not. I haven't heard back from Benoit. Maybe he's decided not to sell at all."

Mischicot took a moment to absorb this thought. "Do we know where Mr. Benoit is staying?"

Both Chaplin and Ramashka shook their heads.

"Well, he must have to lay his head somewhere? Let's find out where that somewhere is and try our little attempt again."

***

Sweeten and his men hurried through the trees until they came to the Square. They then sneaked behind the longhouses, trailers, and municipal buildings. People were working in their gardens, working on their cars, and hanging wash. The deputy told Sweeten that most of the men would be at the river or the bay for hours trying to haul in their daily catches to sell at the market or bring home.

Sweeten stood lookout for anyone possibly heading to the longhouse, but his two men slid in and out with no problem. The next thing he knew, they had the woman kicking, screaming and flinging her arms with a pillowcase over her head as they headed back through the woods.

Sweeten was at the wheel of the SUV when the two men got to the vehicle. Paula was still kicking and fighting. Sweeten nodded to one of his men, who pulled the pillowcase off, slugged her, and knocked her out. He put the pillowcase back over her head. They got in the SUV and it took off.

***

Howard and the group were still assembled in the library when he put his binoculars down.

"Lieutenant Swann, you ride with me. Brett and Kevin, you ride with Callahan. We'll all meet at that cabin where I'm sure they're headed. Brett and Kevin, go the back way. No fire unless I order it. Does everyone understand me?"

Everyone said "yes" in union.

"Agent Watson," Swann said. "Please permit me to get my long gun. It's at my truck at the office."

"Okay, but let's be quick."

Howard then called Marino to update him on the situation.

"What did you just say?" he asked at full volume.

Howard repeated the situation. He needed Marino's approval to do what was necessary from that point on. He got it.

On their drive to Swann's truck, they saw the deputy. Howard had to give Swann some words of advice.

"Lieutenant, bite your lip off if you have to, but don't give away our situation."

They rode past the deputy, and Swann tipped his hat to him. The deputy tipped his hat back and walked in a different direction than the one Howard and Swann were going. The deputy did not look back.

"Nothin' worse than a greedy person," Swann said. "When I get back, before I fire his no-good ass and throw it into prison, I will kick it down the street first!"

Howard understood Swann's words clearly.

When they got to Swann's truck, he lifted his back seat and took out his long gun, which everyone else would call a sniper rifle. He smiled at Howard when he got back in the car.

"Let's go," he said.

***

Sweeten drove as if he wasn't in a hurry. The operation went off without a hitch, he paid the deputy, and his men, and now he was going to get paid big time from Mischicot. He looked ahead to see only one vehicle at the cabin—Ramashka's. He pulled in. One of his men picked up Paula out of the SUV like she was a rag doll and took her into the cabin. She was starting to emerge from unconsciousness.

Ramashka, Mischicot, and especially Chaplin looked at the scene in amazement.

"Is she dead?" Chaplin asked.

"No," Sweeten answered. "Just knocked out. What's next?"

Before Chaplin could answer, the sound of someone on a megaphone outside and the two sedans shielding law enforcement officers was almost too much for Chaplin. She started pacing wildly.

"I told you, Seffy, we shouldn't have come!"

***

Lieutenant Swann looked over at Howard and gave him the megaphone.

Howard held up his credentials so those in the cabin would see them.

"This is the FBI! We have the house surrounded. If you come out with your hands up and with Dr. Malloy, you are guaranteed life at this time. Up to you!"

No sign of any movement came from the house. Howard motioned to Kevin and Brett to go around the back. He was adamant. "No fire unless you're returning it. Understand?"

Both nodded.

Suddenly, Sweeten was on the porch with a gun to Paula's head. She looked vacant.

"Is this who you're looking for? If so, you kill me, and my men will kill her. Up to you."

Howard did not give his statement any power. He motioned to Callahan to go around the back in the opposite direction of Brett and Kevin.

"Swann, how good are you with that long gun?"

"Well, Agent Watson, in Afghanistan, they called me, among other things, a sniper. Who do you want me to pick off first?"

Howard issued another statement on the megaphone. "Andrew Sweeten, this is your last chance to release Dr. Malloy. You must be crazy if you think your people will kill Dr. Malloy. You and your comrades will not survive this day if you in any way hurt her."

The next surprise was when one of Sweeten's men

stepped out on the porch with a gun to Chaplin's head. Sweeten smiled at the latest strategy.

"FBI, you now have two reasons to step aside and let us leave. Up to you."

Sweeten's thug then cocked his gun. Before any more monologues were spit out, Mischicot ran out on the porch and tried to wrestle the gun out of the thug's hand holding Chaplin. The wrestling only lasted a few seconds but the gun went off, and Chaplin's body went limp and fell down the porch steps. The second thug ran out on the porch and aimed his weapon at Mischicot, but Callahan shot the gun out of his hand and both thugs ran back in the house. Sweeten then shot Callahan.

Lieutenant Swann aimed and instantly knocked the life out of Sweeten by shooting him in the head. Paula fell from his grip and also fell down the porch steps. Lieutenant Swann ran over, helped her up from the ground, and walked her to one of the vehicles.

***

Brett and Kevin busted into the cabin, and Ramashka and Sweeten's men held their hands in the air. They were immediately cuffed and led to one of the sedans, where they were put in the backseat. Mischicot ran down the porch steps to Chaplin, held her in his arms, and watched her light go out. On his way to the sedan, Ramashka saw Mischicot holding Chaplin's dead body and looked away quickly.

Howard rushed to Callahan and noticed a lot of blood coming from her right shoulder. He took off his jacket and wrapped it around her shoulder as a tourniquet. It became soaked immediately.

"I'm getting a chopper for you, Callahan. Don't say a word."

***

Swann called the Calvert County Helicopter Emergency Services and provided the coordinates of the village square. He and Howard drove Callahan quickly back to the Square, where the helicopter was promised to arrive within fifteen minutes. Howard was worried because Callahan had lost quite a bit of blood, but he hoped he could bring a smile to her face when he later told her that she was a hero.

Swann watched the villagers circle around his deputy, who was trying hard to dodge their shovels and rocks. Swann pondered a long minute whether he should look the other way. He couldn't do it.

"All right, folks, nothing here to make you this mad. Go back to your homes, gardens, or whatever you were doing because he's not worth you tearing him apart."

One man shouted, "He's a traitor! He threw that innocent woman under the bus for some money!"

Another man shouted, "No telling what he would do next to one of us! I say stone him!"

The crowd agreed with the man.

"What are you going to do, Lieutenant?" Howard asked.

Swann shook his head and walked to the circle with his long gun on his shoulder and stood next to where the deputy slumped on the ground, bleeding.

"Okay, folks, that's enough. I know you're mad, but you're mostly disappointed, especially in someone who made a true and honest commitment under oath that he would not be so greedy that he would take a fee, gift, or bribe. This madness is not us. This madness is not who we are. Just remember, even though we have the power to prosecute tribal citizens on tribal lands, our deputy here committed several *felonies*, so we don't get the chance to stone him. The Federal Government gets to exercise that honor. So, folks, go home, know that Dr. Malloy is now safe, and the people looking to hurt her are either dead or will be in jail for a long time. Go on home now. I'm sure she will be forever grateful to everyone who came out here to see this Judas get that which he deserves, but let the law hang him, not you. Go on now."

The crowd disbursed…slowly. The deputy picked himself up and dusted off his uniform.

"Thanks, Lieutenant, for probably saving my life. I thought they were going to kill me."

At that moment, Swann handed Howard his long gun. He then slapped cuffs on the deputy. "What do you want me to do with this pond scum, Agent Watson?"

"You can throw him in the backseat of my car for now, Lieutenant. I've ordered reinforcements which should be here pretty soon, and they'll take all these parasites out of here."

***

It didn't take long but finally the helicopter landed, and while the EMTs provided emergency medical care to Callahan, Howard got busy signing several documents on her behalf. Afterward, they placed her on a stretcher and lifted her into the bird, taking off.

Two ambulances passed the village a few minutes later on their way to the cabin. Howard had Brett and Kevin supervise the loading of Chaplin's and Sweeten's bodies, providing closure to the operation.

Lieutenant Swann walked over to Howard and offered him his hand. Howard took it.

"You broke the mold, Agent Watson. You broke the mold."

He then walked away with his long gun on his shoulder.

Once reinforcements arrived and Brett and Kevin returned to the Square, Dr. Tanaka told Howard, "That time has come. She is ready to talk."

***

Dr. Tanaka held Paula's hand as the others stood or sat near her.

"Do you know your name?" she began.

Paula looked at everyone in the room. She glanced at Billy and then tried brushing her hair with her hands into a ponytail not realizing the grandmother had already done it for her. She then buttoned the top button on her blouse.

"Paula…Paula Malloy."

"What do you do for a living, Paula Malloy?"

"I am a material sciences technologist for the US Army."

"What are you presently working on?"

"Tony and I…"

She stopped talking. Her eyes widened. She looked at Billy again. She looked at Marty. She seemed to be searching for something as she rubbed her hands continuously. "That guy Sweeten and two different Black guys who looked like wrestlers came to our lab one Friday evening as the guards were changing shifts. Sweeten had to have paid off one of the guards to get to us. They wanted the microchip that Tony and I had just developed. We were taking it to the patent office the following Monday. But we had already put it in the safe like we do every evening Monday through Friday for almost three years. We then communicate to Redstone Arsenal in Alabama that the chip is in the safe. Alabama then confirms with us that they see the disc in the safe."

Dr. Tanaka nodded to Howard.

"Dr. Malloy, I am FBI Special Agent Howard Watson

and would like to ask you a few questions and you can take all the time in the world to answer, is this okay with you?"

She nodded, looking at her hands, now folded in her lap.

"What did Sweeten do next?" Howard asked.

"We told Sweeten the chip was in the bolted-down safe, and we can't get in until Monday morning. He didn't believe us. Sweeten nodded to one of his men, who hit Tony with his gun and kept demanding the combination to the safe. We told them we didn't know the combination. Only Alabama knows it and they provide a new combination to us each morning, and that's how we open the safe. We close it each night, and it does not open again until Monday morning."

She paused.

"They hit Tony again, and when I screamed for them to stop hitting him, they hit me. Then they tied our hands behind us and placed electrical tape over our mouths. We were put into laundry bags and pushed down the laundry chute of our building where a van was waiting. We must have been riding for about an hour when the van finally stopped. When they took the laundry bags off of us, the next thing we both knew we were in some cabin in the woods."

"Would you be able to describe this cabin?"

"Even though it was dark when we arrived, I believe it was the same one I was in today."

"Go on."

"I had to go to the bathroom but the men told me they would not help me, so I went to the toilet in that cabin. Sweeten shouted at me to hurry it up! When I returned to the chair, this time they tied me to it like Tony. I looked over at Tony, who had a busted lip and swollen eyes. I started crying. They told me to shut up. They kicked Tony's glasses down some stairs, and I screamed that they were hurting him. When Sweeten hit me again, my glasses also went down those stairs."

"What about Dr. Serrano?"

"They wouldn't let Tony pee, so he had to pee on himself. I called them cowards. Sweeten told me if I said another word, my family would find me floating face-down in the Chesapeake."

"How did you two get away, Dr. Malloy?"

She hung her head. "They went outside to talk to somebody on the phone, and Tony was able to chew the tape off his mouth. He told me under no circumstances tell them about our failsafe keys. Because even if we give them the keys now, we had seen their faces, and they were going to kill us unless we get out of here."

She stopped talking.

"Take your time, Dr. Malloy. Somebody get her some water."

Brett brought her a glass of water, which she immediately drank.

She continued. "Tony was able to replace the tape over his mouth, not exactly like before, but the kidnappers didn't notice. They didn't worry about us because they had tied us to our chairs with our wrists bound behind us. The men decided to get something to eat but told us not try anything and they would return."

"Once we saw their vehicle's lights blurred, Tony tried untying the rope around my chair. It took more than a minute. I was about to undo his rope when suddenly the vehicle returned. Tony yelled at me, to run, run as fast as I could, that he could handle this. Just keep running until it was light. 'Tell Steven that I love him.'"

She bowed and shook her head. "I told him I couldn't. I told him I couldn't leave him. Oh, Tony. I can't leave you. But he screamed at me to 'Go! Go now!'"

All eyes in the room were moist.

She looked down at her hands and began rubbing them as if something was on them. Howard took her hands to help her stop.

She continued. "I remember the bathroom had a window over the toilet, so I stepped on the toilet and fell out of that window with my hands still tied behind me and the tape still on my mouth, but I ran, and I ran, and I ran. There must have been a moon because I saw a bridge, and as I ran to the bridge, I tripped and fell. The next thing I recall I was waking up on this couch."

Paula's tears flowed like a waterfall. Although she knew the answer, she still asked about Tony. After being given the details, the waterfall repeated itself.

"He saved my life!" she cried. "Tony saved my life."

She looked for Billy, who held her until the tears stopped flowing.

***

Both teams met in Fleischman's conference room. Agent Callahan and her supervisor from Quantico were also among the noisy group. Callahan's right arm was in a pink cast and sling; all the agents signed it. Fleischman's executive assistant was instrumental in keeping out the press. After he felt more than enough time had transpired for coffee and conversation, Fleischman began the meeting.

"People, what we have accomplished in the past four weeks has been remarkable, from uncovering the truth about two wonderful and accomplished kidnapped American scientists, to erasing the manufactured facades of irresponsible business people in our community. These same people we have held in high esteem were so desperate in their greed that it brought down their empire."

He paused. "Al, how about you and Gerry taking it from here?"

Marino was quite shocked that Fleischman had said as much as he did because he had yet to hear the complete details of the operation from him or Gerry.

"Working together," Marino began, "we accomplished our mission, which was two-fold: to find our two scientists and to make sure Boris Ramashka, Sebastien Mischicot, and Carla Chaplin went to prison. Unfortunately, we didn't anticipate any deaths. Actually, we didn't anticipate any fire at all. But this is the world we live in and the job we have chosen to uphold. Agent Watson was genuinely instrumental in leading our group. His piecing together Dr. Serrano's death and the Piscataway Indian Nation is what led us to recover Dr. Malloy. Agent Millhouse was undoubtedly influential with his Baltimore team, but Gerry can speak to that."

Everyone around the table nodded in agreement.

"However, I would be remiss if we did not acknowledge the creative and genius world of Agent Waverly and what he accomplished in a fixed amount of time. Although the operation was scrubbed, Ahmad reminded us why we have him on board."

Howard and Tim could not control themselves so they stood up and applauded. Even Fleischman applauded, which made Ahmad grin.

"One last thing," Marino added. "We must recognize and appreciate the clear thinking and quick action of Agent Callahan, who probably saved the life of Dr. Malloy."

The applause made her *and* her supervisor smile.

Marino looked over at Kramer. "Gerry, I'm sure you want to say something."

"Most of you know I'm a man of a few words, but today I have many because Agent Millhouse, who has only been an SSA for less than a year, performed his duties admirably, both on paper and in the execution of Baltimore's part of the operation. His team, and as I found out, Agent Watson's team, has glowing words of appreciation and respect for Terrence. I am pleased to say his promotion to SSA was the correct move for the FBI."

Millhouse wiped the tear from the side of his eye. He stood up and nodded to everyone around the room. He then nodded at Howard. Kramer then glanced briefly at Fleischman, who looked like he was genuinely enjoying the conference. He stood up.

"Thank you all again for your efforts. We will formally acknowledge your teams in three weeks at Academy graduation. Before we adjourn, Al and Gerry, the press is waiting outside these doors, but the rest of you can leave through my office."

Howard returned to his office and called Jim Stanley with the outcome of the operation.

"Wow, Howard," he could only offer. "Wow."

***

December, five months later

Known as the Sixth Nobel Prize, The Nobel Memorial Prize in Economic Sciences was awarded to Dr. Paula Malloy and posthumously to Dr. Antony Serrano "for their outstanding contribution to the field of economics with their proven approach to alleviating global atrocities concerning the elimination of anti-personnel landmines."

The beautiful 24-karat gold coin consisted of Alfred Nobel's likeness on the front and the field for which the laureate was awarded on the back. The coin, encased in velvet, was set in a black protective case. Dr. Paula Malloy and Dr. Antony Serrano's mother and father received the awards at the ceremony in Stockholm, Sweden. The award included a medal and a diploma, and they shared the monetary portion of the prize.

In the same month, the grandparents of Billy Savoy attended his Ph.D. robing ceremony at Purdue University in West Lafayette, Indiana. This marked the first time both grandparents had been off the settlement grounds. Also attending were his friends Martin Sheridan and Dr. Paula Malloy.

After her brush with death, Paula decided to resign her post from the US Army and help Billy and others with the economic end of running and managing a commercial farm. Although her Nobel Prize coin and diploma hang in her parents' den, alongside her sister's and brother's accomplishments, she invested the monetary award she received from Sweden in the Piscataway Nation's commercial organization, which they appropriately named

Intertribal Connection Farm. Billy's financial seminars paid off as he received $250,000 from the USDA's National Institute of Food and Agriculture, which provided farm grants for training, education, and technical assistance.

In addition, Paula applied for and received a $50,000 Beginning Farmer and Rancher Development Grant because she was a person of color and a woman.

***

Boris Ramashka was sentenced to fourteen years in prison for aggravated kidnapping—hiring someone to commit unlawful confinement of a person against their will and motivated by personal gain. Dr. Antony Serrano, the victim, died while being held against his will. In addition, Ramashka received an additional ten years for second-degree kidnapping in the case of Dr. Malloy. The sentences would run concurrently.

Sebastien Mischicot had removal proceedings initiated against him and was deported to France under moral turpitude guidelines. He received a sentence of life imprisonment, the most severe punishment given under French law for aggravated kidnapping which resulted in a death. He didn't care; he believed he received what was coming to him because of Carla Chaplin's death.

All four of Sweeten's men sang like canaries. Two received sentences of twenty years each for kidnapping FBI Agent Ahmad Waverly from a hotel and the two scientists from their place of work, which resulted in a death. The odds were not in their favor for the possibility of a reduced sentence.

The other two men received sentences of ten years each for kidnapping Dr. Malloy from the Piscataway Nation, and with time off for good behavior, they could be looking at five years.

***

Paula and Billy asked Steven Glass if he could provide medical assistance to their farmhands on the Piscataway land once a month, to which he gladly agreed. Antony Serrano's parents offered Steven the Nobel Prize's monetary portion, but he offered an exchange instead— Tony's diploma or Nobel medal. They happily provided him with the medal.

***

July, six months later

Paula's paternal grandfather was 100 percent Creek Indian, so she was quickly able to prove a blood quantum of twenty-seven percent, to all of the Indians' delight. She could now marry Billy Savoy with no issues arising from the clan.

Paula continued to help Marty with his translations and memorizations without asking to be paid, and Marty not only walked down the aisle for his Ph.D. robing ceremony, but he also walked Billy down the aisle as his best man.

Howard, Margaret Tanaka, Steven Glass, Tadeo Tran, Ruby Ha, Sandra Callahan and their families were all invited as part of the celebration of Billy's and Paula's union, which was a combination of the Indian ways and Paula's Baptist upbringing. It seemed everyone who attended from Paula's family and most of the Indians could not believe the similarities in each other. Even Lieutenant Swann and his new deputy enjoyed the delicious meal from two distinct cultures and the diverse music and dancing afterward.

The Intertribal Connection Farm became profitable after only two years. Howard even sent his twins to work on the farm in the summers, where they stayed on the land.

Howard was thankful. Thankful that the operation had ended, and thankful that it ended on a high note.

THE END

JoAnn Fastoff is an award-winning author of both fiction and non-fiction books. She has written for numerous publications, has produced three one-act plays Off-Off-Broadway in New York, and produced and directed *Live from the Warehouse,* a jazz program for several PBS affiliates. Ms. Fastoff is an environmental activist, the mother of two adult children and the grandmother of Lia. She is from Chicago.

The Avaricious is the seventh novel in the Howard Watson Intrigue series. Visit her website at www.JoAnnFastoff.com

www.ingramcontent.com/pod-product-compliance
Lightning Source LLC
Chambersburg PA
CBHW021445150726
47989CB00001B/396